Beyond Death and Other Stories

Beyond Death and Other Stories

Sunil R. P. Sethi

PRABHAT PRAKASHAN

Published by
PRABHAT PRAKASHAN PVT. LTD.
4/19 Asaf Ali Road,
New Delhi-110 002 (INDIA)
e-mail: prabhatbooks@gmail.com

ISBN 978-93-5266-741-3
BEYOND DEATH AND OTHER STORIES
by Sunil R. P. Sethi

Edition
2025

Price
₹ 250.00 (Rupees Two Hundred Fifty only)

Printed at
Shree Sai Printers, Sahibabad

Contents

1. Beyond Death 7
2. Swamiji 13
3. Nafeesa Bi 22
4. Megha And Family 31
5. Choti Maa 36
6. Debt 42
7. Unspoken Friendship 48
8. Umbilical Cord 52
9. Bilqees 56
10. Maryada 60
11. Mother-In-Law 64
12. Keshav 68
13. Airgun 72
14. Inspector 75
15. Hijacker 79
16. Relation Unknown 83
17. Preacher 87
18. Daughter of Water 90
19. Manthra 93

20. Daughter of God 98
21. Mai Bhago 102
22. Queen of Heartz 105
23. Durga 108
24. Breast Tax 111
25. Half and 14 114

1
Beyond Death

Inspector Mukesh was sitting on his chair in police station when a constable brought before him a boy of about 8 years of age. Mukesh was busy reading official files pertaining to case investigations going on in police station. He raised his head from file and asked the constable "Who is this child and why is he in police station." Child was good looking with decent clothing and didn't look like involved in crime, speaking from experience of Mukesh. "Sir please listen to him. He is talking nonsense and has created scene in police station." Mukesh gave a stern look to child and closed file. He indicated chair to child to sit down and asked Constable to bring water for child. "I will take tea and my name is Anand before you ask me." Mukesh had smile on his face at the wit of child and passed signal to constable, who went out.

Mukesh then addressed Anand: "Now tell me in detail whatever you want to say." Anand looked matured and serene by looks, far beyond his age. Suddenly, his face could reflect all pains and agonies going on inside him. Anand said: "I want you to investigate my murder." Mukesh was taken aback. He asked, "Who has been murdered." And answer shocked him no limits "ME." Mukesh looked at Anand but his face reflected pain and he was very serious.

This was turning out to be very interesting and mysterious. Tea had arrived and Anand took cup of tea and started his narrative.

"I was Kumar in my last birth and was living in this very city in Street No. 27 and was killed 11 years back. My dead body was not found and it was presumed that I had run away. My mother waited for me every moment till she died three years back. Her last breath had gone but eyes were wide open, waiting for her son to come even at her last time which never happened as son had already left the world eight years before her "Anand uttered painfully. Mukesh was at the edge of his seat. "Who killed you?" He asked. He was in for a greater shock. Answer was "My wife and my son".

Anand then said: "I was living with my wife Aarti and my 21 years old son Aditya. I was working as supervisor in road construction department and had good salary and also had ancestral land in village which had come in road expansion and I had got compensation of about four crores which was huge amount by our standards. Despite my best efforts my son had fallen in bad company and was thrashed by me when I found him taking drugs on roof one day. I never had good relations with my wife whom I always found greedy and impatient. Now with money coming in abundance both my wife and my son were after me to give money to Aditya so that he can start business. I knew he would waste money as he was good for nothing and would rather go more deep in drug abuse by spending money. It was a rainy night when they both came to me. I could see clearly that Aditya was under influence of drugs with drowsy eyes and blussed face. But I was shocked to find same expression on face of Aarti. Seemed she had also taken some drugs or intoxicant. I lost my cool, may be for first time in life and shouted that I was betrayed by both and I won't tolerate this anymore. I also shouted at them that next morning I will divorce Aarti and disown Aditya. They were both shocked. Aarti threatened me that she would not allow that to happen as she had waited her life for living life of luxury and comfort and wouldn't allow me to throw her on road. Aditya ran inside with rage and came back with kitchen knife. He asked me whether I would still stuck to my decision. I said yes though I knew father in me would compel me to partition money in three equal parts. I wanted to keep one-third of money basically for my old-widowed mother who was living in village and was dependent on me for survival".

Mukesh was becoming impatient to know more. He said: "What happened then." Anand had finished his tea and was looking at Mukesh with question mark on his face. Mukesh called constable and asked him to bring one more tea. Anand continued, "I had said that but I knew Aditya wouldn't harm his father neither Aarti would allow that. But I was wrong. As I turned my back I felt immense pain in my back. I turned around and saw knife stabbed in my back by Aditya who was holding it. He pulled it back. I cried and asked Aarti to stop Aditya and that I would give money. She said money issue had gone now. At this time Aditya again stabbed me and then it was all madness with him inflicting 27 stabs on me and killed his father. After I fell down, I suddenly felt liberated and was flouting in air but saw my body lying in pool of blood on floor. I wanted to cry and shout and call people for neighbourhood but I had no voice however hard I tried. I could only watch. I witnessed ruthless manner in which my body was dismembered by my son and my wife and then burying different parts of my body at three different place in city that night. Next morning story was made by Aarti that I had fight with her and I had left home after executing will in her favour, never to come back. They got what they wanted and I even didn't get decent cremation."

Story looked unbelievable beside it involved Aditya Choudhary a big businessman and politically wellconnected person but there were some apparently believable parts like father of Aditya having gone missing and still untraced. Mukesh took Anand with him and his team and in fact they could find bones at the place where Anand had pointed out. After arrest and in interrogation Aditya and Aarti confessed everything. What Anand was saying was true, absolutely true. Anand wanted to slap his both murderers which Mukesh agreed, though it was not legal, but then, what Aarti and Aditya had done deserved punishment more than what law would give them. But when time came to slap them in police lock up, Anand failed again. He could only ask Aarti and Aditya "Why? What was my fault?" And then he felt tears rolling down, which couldn't come when he left body and saw the most heinous crime. Aarti and Aditya were so moved that they agreed to make confession before magistrate, which was only way to get their conviction as there was no evidence otherwise.

Next day Mukesh was again sitting in police station with a satisfied looking matured eight years old boy sitting across table holding cup of tea. Mukesh asked, "where would you go now? Shall, I drop you to your home?" Anand replied "I don't know. I have no home or family." Mystery was still not leaving and thus the new curiosity for Mukesh. "From where have you come?" Anand smiled and said, "leave it as you won't believe." Mukesh looked clueless but he said "Do try. You have reached so far as only I could believed you."

So Anand again started over tea "After I moved away from home I went through a tunnel which had very soothing light and while passing through it my all worries, bad feelings, anger and pains were getting washed off. I was feeling free and light as a feather. Time had no relevance. I always wanted to remain like that but after process of apparent cleansing I again found myself in womb of my new mother and was born in due times and grew up in my new home" Mukesh got some relief at least from his mysteries. "Where is your home? Let me call your parents." Anand smiled, "You can't call them. None can." Mukesh said "Oh Are they no more?" Anand said, "They are alive and healthy but beyond your reach and contemplation." Again new mystery had started. Before Mukesh could ask Anand started.

"I took birth not in this world or even this universe. That was another universe where almost everything is same. Same type of humans and vehicles and buildings and progress but physical laws are little different." Mukesh was again shocked. He asked, "Like what?" Anand smiled, "Like we don't feel hunger or fell sick. We remember all past lives and live with our relatives or known out of our choice. We have no fight and no government as there are no nations but only one nation." Mukesh asked, "What about religion and which god you follow?" Anand replied, "we don't believe in concept of religion or even god. That's process of evolution and in future even your earth would need no god. Process of million gods to One and then NONE. And this series of Universes have no end. Each successive universe having more evolved laws of physics and also human beings. Travel to our universe from more evolved parallel universes is very common but not so to your universe as going back is difficult. In our universe, a person choose his death when his all desires are over and he is ready for higher planes. There are no animals as we don't need them."

Mukesh was stunned. The whole life circle stood unfolded before him, even beyond the concepts of creation so far known. His inner hunger was unsatiated. He asked, "How you came here?"Anand looked visibly disturbed. With pain in voice he said: "When my mother came to our world and met me, I came to know about her sufferings. And by the way we don't communicate through words. We can read each other's mind so there is only truth existing. I felt rage which was unusual in my world and I wanted to come to teach lesson to perpetrators of crime not only against me but also my mother who was not taken care of and who died as beggar. When I told my community leader he was annoyed and said that I may never come back. But I was insistent and so I got transported here when in sleep. I have no idea how to go back or whether I will ever go back to meet my family. Now, I realise my mistake in taking revenge. I can't live here as I remember everything and I can't go there as I am clueless in that." He stood to move out of room. Mukesh finally asked, "But your name sounded Hindu, Anand." Smilingly was answer given "we have no names as we don't need them either. That was only for you so that we can communicate." Off he went leaving behind a visibly shaken and new Avatar of Mukesh. He was never heard of again. May be he found his way back or may be he is still wandering and trying to find one.

❐

2
Swamiji

City was on festivity. Streets were decorated and there were big hoardings welcoming Swami Prakash to the city. He was visiting city personally after 12 years, though his followers had been following his teachings and listening to his recorded sermons on television. For last seven years, he was in meditation and had not spoken a word and he has chosen his city of birth to speak for first time after long meditation. His followers are spread all over the world and may be more than five millions. Everyone was curious to listen to Swamiji for his words of wisdom.

He arrived on the day to his Ashram and was taken in huge procession to Prade Ground where huge crowd of not less than 50 thousand people had come to listen to son of city who had risen to be one of top spiritual leaders of the world and who had his communes and Ashrams throughout the world and who had done so much for his city. A small insignificant city some 30 years ago is now centre to education for whole Northen India and also industrial hub, thanks to the extensive works done by society of Swamiji. His follower Seth Jamna Dass has started construction of his huge diamond polishing plant which will be commissioned next year and will change the development scenario of Prema Nagar which most of population wants to change to Swami Prakash Nagram but Swamiji always refused.

Sitting on dias Swamiji choose two small kids from crowd to sit on his either side, one boy and one girl. They would share Das with Swamiji for rest of day or as long as they can sit. It was great honour bestowed upon the kids and a learning and transforming experience. They knew from that day onwards their life will change as also the way people take them.

After his discourse on spiritualism and the ways of religion to realise God, Swamiji invited public to ask any question to him. That was the highlight of the function his followers always wait for. These interactions always lead to getting instructions from the master himself about the way to live life and experience God while living normal life. The first person to ask questions was Nilakant, university scholar and social work who had insatiable hunger of path of God Realisation. He asked "What is Religion Swamiji?" Smilimgly came the answer "Any thought process which brings you to path of Self-Realisation, of understanding the reason for taking birth, of appreciating way of life." Further question was "Can we understand God without religion?" Swamiji answered with his well-known Grace "You don't need religion at all to understand god or godliness. God realisation is much beyond religions. It's personal effort where everything has to evaporate except realisor and the realised. Religion only put you on path. It's starting point but beyond that religion has little scope. In fact, Great men and women who started different religions are best examples of finding God without religions. It is again not necessary that you can always find start through religions only. Start can also be through personal effort, though a bit difficult but at the same time if a person get immersed in religious dogmas, he will also not reach anywhere beyond a mere start. Religion is great distractions."

Anandi, a housewife was next to stand up to ask her questions. She had been a dutiful wife and mother and hardly could get time even to go to temple regularly. She asked with folded hands "Swamiji can I realise the Truth only by doing my duties towards all relations and to rest of

Humanity?" Swami Prakash Ji replied, "Living a righteous life and performing duties towards all is necessary to be good and useful and that in a way is best preparation for purifying yourself before entering house of God which dwells in all of us, but merely being good wife or mother or human being won't be sufficient to know the truth. While you do good to all, be good to yourself too by investing in yourself. Find time to understand yourself and through it you will understand the whole nature and existence." Anandi had tears in her eyes. Her Swamiji could so easily read her inner turmoil. With folded hands she sat down having found her way of salvation.

Yusuf was next to stand up. He said Salam alaikum to Swamiji with all respect. Swamiji smiled and raising his right hand to his forehead in Islamic way said Walekum assalam. Yusuf was a butcher and had remained in jail for about seven years in a murder case and hot transformed after joining Swamiji. "Does God loves also person who has committed crime?" He asked. Swamiji understood the inner fights of Yusuf and replied: "God is more like mother than father. He doesn't abandon his children even if children wants to forget him. For him all are equal. Victims as well as assailants but everyone has to pay for his wrongs. You have to atone the crime committed and come clean thereafter. There is nothing like getting amnesty after committing crime. No amount of going to religious places or performing any procedure provided by so-called religions will wash away the stains of crimes. Whether you go to Kashi or Kabba or Jersulam or Kailash, your deeds will follow you always. You are carrying the burden on your mind which is with you even after death. But if you change and be good that will surely lessen the punishment." Yusuf asked, "What about punishment a person get from courts. Isn't it punishment enough?" Swamiji replied, "That is punishment to body who commits crime. Body or mind or both. What about punishment to mind? That can be done only by changing mind for good or your mind and soul will continue suffering even after death." Yusuf had knew more question "Swamiji' is a butcher different than a priest in the eyes of God?" Reply came "This is a brilliant question Yusuf. Many have doubt on this. I say to you there is no difference between two in eyes of God. For Him all are equal and same. You can continue with your profession but act with mercy and not hatred. Even when you are killing an animal as part of your way to earn don't leave compassion out of your mind. God require pure mind not bodies. A priest who look after temple or mosque or curch or gurudwara but with unclean mind Which is infested with vices and malice is worst creature for God".

Next in line was Murli, a software engineer and a self-proclaimed atheist who believed in Charvak way of philosophy, the belief in materialism only, the world existing as the parameters of Nature leaves no other option. There was no God as there was no necessity to create him. He stood up and asked with a voice bolstering of self-pride more than faith, pride that he knew more than other and with a desire to make Swamiji realise that Murli had better knowledge than Swamiji. "Don't you think we created God and not vice versa?" Swamiji was equally comfortable and replied, "You may not be incorrect though I can't say you are correct. Ultimate aim of existence is to understand the purpose of existence and if concept of God can help you in that I don't find anything wrong in that. Besides even if I believe in materialism as Mahrishi Charvak taught and which is now followed by most of world across all religions, I am still left with one basic unanswered question, can there be creation without a Creator? Can there be effect without a cause? You believe in science so believe in laws of motion of Newton. First law is on principle of Inertia. Things don't move unless a force is applied. Whether you call that force Nature or God it will mean same. Name is not important. Even if you change names the truth of a creator will always remain staring at you. Murli was speechless. He still asked, first time with folded hands "Swamiji where am I wrong?" Reply came "Knowledge is to know not to boost. When you get knowledge use it to improve yourself and not to tell others that you are superior. Don't try to become different. It's good for a leaf to flow with stream to reach ocean, if you be different you will be pushed to shores and will rot there."

Rishi, student in college was next to stood up. He was studious and had always stood first in studies and besides was also given to sports with cricket as his passion. He had been following different sects, absorbing best of all but still not satisfied. He asked: "How should we treat our parents?" Answer was "Same way you want to be treated by your children when you will grow old." Next question "And how should we treat our children?" And answer "Same way you always expected your parents to treat you." Rishi had come prepared with his volley of questions. He asked: "How should we treat friends?" Swamiji said "Treat them with love and regards and value them greatly. You chose them and not accident of your birth. Don't make any promise which you can't fullfill and don't test them unless very necessary." Rishi asked "What about strangers?" Answered Samiji "Meet them with humility. You should have straight and not stiff neck. It's always good to bow and be flexible." Rishi had one last one "When should we leave truth and speak lie?" Swamiji said "Though generally keep your life simple and straight where you don't need to tell lie but if your lie can help general good and speaking truth in situation will create harm to others, it may be resorted to without saying a word more than what is required."

That was end of session one. Time for lunch. Everyone else with Swamiji, who gave his fingers of either hands to two kids who would get honour to have food with him.

Swamiji slept for some times after lunch and by 3 pm he was ready what was going to be Intense Sessions for discourse, where the questions on deep spiritual knowledge was asked by people already initiated as distinct from first sessions where people seeking guidance and answers were mainly people living normal household lives. It was the second sessions which results in discourses of higher understandings and which would be reproduced in book form as well as audio-video presentations.

After Swamiji settled down on dias, he looked at the audience. Now only people already initiated were left who would seek to clear their doubts. They were all on path of liberation and had reached some distance. First to ask questions was Swami Surya lovingly called Chote Swamiji, he was favourite disciple of Swamiji and had imbibed the qualities of his Guru and was looking after the welfare projects of the commune. "What is truth of Death? Is it end of life?" Chote Swamiji asked. With customary smile Swamiji closed his eyes and replied: "Death is a myth. It doesn't exist. Nothing dies. Death is just an extended sleep. There is nothing to be afraid of Death or even be perturbed. Do you enjoy your sleep?" "Yes I do." Replied Chote Swamiji. "Are you afraid of sleep Surya?" "No Swamiji because I know I will wake up again. There is some amount of certainty in waking up again, though not an absolute one." Swamiji was impressed. He always liked talking to Surya as he could anticipate coming questions and answer them before hand. Swamiji continued "So if you know you will still rise after death, all fear will be gone. Now listen carefully.

Nothing in this world ever get destroyed. Everything remains. That's what science says and that's what religion also says. It's not on many things they agree." Surya asked: "Could you explain Swamiji." Swamiji replied: "Theory of Relativity says nothing can be created nor destroyed but they can change form. It's all game between matter and energy. They interchange their positions and that's what creates everything around. But their is third dimension too conciousness which bring order to matter and energy and whose capacity and capabilities are yet being tapped. So nothing will ever die. After death only form will be changed. Religion also says same. None had ever lived and none has ever died, this is all game of Maya that is consciousness. We exist in simulation and not in real time. You can see a person dying but not death as there is no such nothing. There is no end. When a child grows and become young man, it is not that child had died. He will exist in young person. Similarly, you will live in something else but that won't end you. If you understand this the whole game will be clear to you."

Acharya Agnivesh asked next question: "Swamiji, Does God really exist? Is everything created by God or it existed by itself?" This question had always come to Swamiji in all previous assemblies too in one form or other and each time he had to reply in different way depending upon person who wants answer. He looked in the deep eyes of Agnivesh who had chosen path of spiritualism after doing his post graduation in physics. Swamiji said: "Agnivesh can there be effect without cause?" "No Swamiji. There has to be cause for the effect as per principle of Inertia." "So when even a leaf can't be moved without some force moving how can there be such a vast creation without a creator. If you believe everything to have come into existence without external force then you have to leave all logic. Your science will stop at big bang. What about existence before that and then before that. One absurdity will lead to series of uncertainties. Of course, definition and understanding of God or Creator may differ. Definition may be changed but not existence. If we believe your science which now says nothing exist in real time not even time itself then this whole existence is Maya only and God will be creator of Maya. Existence of God brings certainty to many questions, though some may still remain unexplained mostly because of limitations of our perceptions but nonexistence of God will lead to most of questions unanswered. "Swamiji then said laughingly. It is better to believe in God till we find something better to believe in Vinita Ji was next to stood up. She was heading the women organisation of commune. "Swamiji what is true love?" Swamiji folded his hands and said "True love is knowing that nobody is apart from you and you are part of everyone. Everything around you is your extension and vice versa. So treat all as you are treating yourself." Seeing question mark in eyes of Vinita Ji, Swamiji continued: "Every thing in the existence is having same constituents. Whether living or non-living the building blocks of everything are atoms and sub-atomic particles are same in everything. So everything is created from same. Moulds may be different. What is in me is also in you and vice versa. Where are we different? Whom to hate and be angry with. It's you everywhere. Even God will be same, your extension or in other words you and everything around is his extension. Be at peace with everyone and love everyone." Vinita Ji asked: "Swamiji in worldly physical sense we tend to control persons we love. Is it justified?" "Not at all. Love is feeling for giving someone everything. When you are in true love, you want the object of your love to be happy and it matters not what it takes. If you wish to possess the person you love or wants him to be only concerned about you then it is not love at all. In love you give freedom and surrender yourself without regard or expectations of return."

Next in line was Anand, the young Sanyasi. He asked "Swamiji how important is prayer in meditations?"

Replied Swamiji: "It is the most important thing in any kind of meditation or spiritualism that there should be total surrender. When surrender is total, the path is lighted so prayer is important aspect as it denotes surrender. Prayer may be silent or in words spoken, that matters not. Power of prayers are immense as it can lead to results which are inconceivable by logic. The genius Indian mathematician Ramanuja, a very mediocre student, could solve mathematical problems which even best mathematician of the world couldn't contemplate. Some of his theories could be understood after 40 years of his death and he did so just by sitting in silent prayer and all answers would happen to him. Similarly during Second World War Hitler put reward of one million marks on Masson Wolfe who had the capacity to change conscious of others just by his prayers. If you ask me the extent of powers of prayers, I will say INFINITY.

Master Ayub was the next person to ask. Chote Swamiji announced that it would be last question of the day. Ayub asked "Swamiji what's the easiest way to find God? In prayers or in fast or in temple, mosques or church, or in reading Holy books or serving poor?" Swamiji said: "In none of above. God is knowledge and you have to acknowledge. These are to improve ways of life but won't help you to understand or find God. Do you really want to meet God?" "Yes Swamiji." Everyone else sitting also was attentive. "Ayub drop yourself and see God in front of you standing as a true friend. To meet him you have to drop all your clothing of ego and teachings and even consciousness. Drop everything and just flow in the stream and let him take your hands and move you with him. But remember he likes no wordly clothes sewn by you from your vices. Once you meet him naked, he will never leave you and will never allow you wear clothes again. You don't have to wait for years to meet and understand him. It can happen just now. Only one moment is all that is needed. May you get peace and love".

That was the end of Deep Session as also of the day. Swamiji stood up from his seat and everyone chanted.

— Shanti Shanti Shanti Swami
— Nirmal Chit Anand Swami

❐

3
Nafeesa Bi

She looked at the mirror to see her face full of wrinkles, the time has left and with pain and agony clearly writ large in the eyes which had seen so much. She wondered, with which ink, her life story had been written by God. Even, stones would be in tears and mountains would melt on listening to what she has gone through. What she had lived though was no life, it was Hell, pure Hell! Looking back at the dead body of her husband, lying on bed, she looked up in the skies. This moment had come her way by destiny. How she wished she could have caused it to happen herself. What had died was the tormentor of her life, the person who made each moment of her life a living hell and then he was father of her children whom she loved, though they were born out of hatred. Her life flashed back.

She was born as Verranwati to a wealthy and respected landlord and moneylender of the city Mirpur. She was the eldest child of the family and much pampered. As her name goes, she was followed by two brothers and she was a doting sister especially for youngest Narayan. After independence, her state was a princely state which had Muslim majority but a Hindu king who decided, after much deliberations and political upheavals, to accede to India which lead to situations that changed her life.

In the events that followed, her peaceful city which had always been taken as symbol peaceful coexistence of different religious thinking and whose name itself was synthesis of two great religious preggers of the city of different religions, was torn apart with large influx of outsiders, mostly Tribals. Leaders of city, including her father, however felt assured as state forces unit, with arms and ammunition, was stationed there and would check any misadventure, as per assurance of, head of, district administrations, Rattan Singh, who was the relative of the king. Her father gave a huge amount to administration to ensure safety and security to all residents and in fact, created a small group of sound persons of both communities to defend city from communal backlash as had happened in Punjab. She was 11 years old and her brothers were 5 years and 7 years younger to her. She took training to use him or her father if time so come.

Then it started one night. Large number of intruders entered the city armed with firearms. She heard they include regular army personal in civil of Pakistan. That night the resistance group created by her father stood up and repulsed the attack with some support from state forces. In morning they counted dead bodies of seven intruders and one village boy. Situation suddenly had become tense and it was obvious that attack would happen again and again. She heard her father telling Rattan Singh, in a meeting held at her Haveli, to call Indian army which was only 20 miles away in Jhangar. Rattan Singh promised that Indian Army would come next day. While village stood reassured and slept in peace. Nothing happened that night.

She couldn't however sleep whole night and was looking out of the window of her Haveli, the only three-storey building of the town with red flag atop declaring that building owner was a Millionaire, a big thing those days. Out she saw Drabu Khan, the mad man, who was always roaming around in the streets and was filthy and abusive and roughine who was looked down by everyone. She remembered when he followed her for few days some two years back, how mercilessly he was thrashed by the police and by her father. He didn't dare to even look towards her thereafter. But tonight he was staring at her Haveli. She could see a different Drabu who was looking aggressive. She saw many people moving out of the town that night discreetly though she couldn't identify them. Truth came out next morning only.

Town woke up in winterly chilled morning to find to their horrors that Rattan Singh and whole contingent of the state forces had run away in the darkness of night abandoning the town and inhabitants to the mercy of invaders. That was act of extreme cowardice and back stabbing otherwise the people would have moved out of town a day before. Now all escape routes were plugged and all inhabitants were holed up. Any chance of outside help had vanished as state forces with Rattan Singh had taken away the single wireless set, the only source of communication with outside world and Indian Army who was only 20 miles away but had not moved an inch towards them even though news of genocide being underway must had reached them. It was no time to curse the leaders who were responsible for keeping the army on hold and looming towards large population of Mirpur as spectators only. Humanity had died. Army could be moved to save Kashmir but not Mirpur. Strange are ways of politics. The whole population had gathered in Haveli of her father who had opened gates of his godowns and provided all needy people whatever was required and whatever was him. Hour of distress had brought brotherhood on the fore.

Next day the invaders entered the city and there was total commotion. She hid in her store on top floor. The little resistance, the guards of her father could provide, ended by afternoon and then she saw dance of death. Drabu was moving in her verandah like a ragged bull. Blood dropping from his sword was testimony to the horrific deeds which must had been performed by the beast. And then what happened, hounded her for all her remaining life, if it can call that. To her full view, Drabu dragged her father and beheaded him. He then stabbed his brother to death.

Thereafter, he picked the youngest one by legs and was about to bang him on floor when she ran screaming to save him. Alas! the effort failed. Before she could reach him, Drabu had banged the head of her youngest brother on the floor and his face was destroyed beyond recognition. She saw her mother being dragged inside the room by two demons and then screams of her, before she fell unconscious.

Regaining consciousness, she found herself in a dirty hut with hands and feet tied. Drabu entered after sometime. His face was covered in blood and he looked like butcher. She asked weeping, "Where is my mother?" Laughed the demon, "She has been taken whose reward she was. You are my reward." Then she felt lifeless as life force in her had left. Thereafter, what was raped by Drabu was a dead body, cold flesh. She could only remember words of her father "You will live on." That was curse for her.

In coming weeks and months, her body was tortured by her tormentor Drabu and subjected to ravishing. She forgot numbers. Her town had become part of Pakistan in so called Azad state. Drabu was awarded 18 biggas of land and princely sum of five hundred for act of bravery in killing 13 kafirs and keeping daughter of leader of ladies with him. He built his house and then one day she was converted by Molvi and got married to same demon Drabu. Her consent for Nikkah was never there and now she said yes but her silence was taken as yes by Molvi and she was married to person who she hated most in life.

In the hours of time she became mother of two daughters and three sons. Her two sons died in infancy. The only surviving son was Anwar. Whenever she saw her children, she could feel intense hatred for Drabu but then, mother in her overcame her intense hatred for father of children and she could feel softening in her burning eyes only when she saw Anwar. She always saw her brother, Narayan, in him whom Drabu killed in most inhuman way by banging him on the floor. Many a times, she thought of putting poison in food of Drabu to take revenge for her family but then, face of Anwar always made her to desist as, killing Drabu would have lead to her being sent to jail and she couldn't think of living without Anwar for a moment though, never did a moment came when she forgot what happened before eyes on that 28th Nov. Nafeesa was attached to daughters Sahiba and Nadira though, not as much as Anwar. They were married by Drabu when they were about 18 years and 17 years respectively. Drabu didn't even think it necessary to discuss marriages with her. She was just informed at the last moment of impending marriages of both daughters in single function with nephews of Drabu and given money to do marriage shopping. Both girls wanted to study and pleaded with her to talk to their father but she remembered the face of Drabu on that day when he killed her family. And she remained mum. Her only respite was that Anwar was equally attached to her and for him whatever his mother ordered was to be complied as command of God. Anwar was good in studies and passed secondary school in first grade. He always wanted to join army. Though, Nafeesa was fearful of Anwar going to army but she never wanted to see disappointment in eyes of her only reason to live. She smilingly gave her consent. Drabu opposed and scolded Anwar and even raised his hand but Anwar was stout young man of 18 years and Drabu was not as strong as he was 30 years back. Consent of mother was what mattered for Anwar. Drabu didn't have guts to ask her to stop Anwar.

When Anwar got selected for Army Defence Academy, the whole locality came to congratulate her. It was there, she met Nahid for the first time. She was almost of same age as Nafeesa and was working as teacher in local primary school. Her husband had died and she had one daughter who was studying in Matriculation. In short time they became close friends. Nafeesa got a friend for first time in life. Nahid's story was no different either. She was only 7 years old when her whole family was murdered before her eyes on the bridge of River Chinab. And the person who murdered her whole family was just a boy of 17 or 18 years of age. He was of course part of a crowd. All captured persons, including females, were made to stand on bridge and then after beheading, the bodies were thrown in river to go to their Pakistan. She had never heard of Pakistan before. She alongwith whole family was taken from their village in Reasi for "safe and secure place". And this was done by the village Numberdar, Jaipal Singh, whom she had always called and treated as Chacha and her family was murdered on the bridge by son of same Chacha Jaipal Singh. When her turn came for being butchered, the hands of her murderer must have shaken looking in her eyes. She got a big slash of sword on her shouldér and was thrown in river Chinab. Ice cold water of Chinab washed her wound and froze her blood before she fell unconscious only to regain her consciousness in a refugee camp in areas under control of Pakistan. She heard in camp itself about number of headless bodies coming from river. Inhumanity everywhere.

But then, she saw face of God. Molvi Tari adopted 13 hapless children who arrived from river alive and took them to local Masjid where a part was then converted as their residence. Molvi was father figure to all and was full of compassion. Because of his reputation and conduct, there was never problem in funds gathering for upbringing the kids. She studied and got her graduation and then was married to Zaman who was working as Engineer in Mangla Dam. Her life was smooth now but never a day passed when she was not woken from sleep from nightmare of horrific incident on the bridge. She again saw kindness of her God when she was blessed with daughter Anjum. Life had taken a full turn and she thought nothing bad can happen to her now.

But destiny had its own plan. Zaman, who had been very kind and loving to her, met with an accident and died when Anjum was only 4 years old. She was shattered but had to stand strong, atleast for Anjum. She was given job as teacher because of death of her husband while on duty. And this started her struggle to sustain in life with self respect. Living alone with minor daughter was not easy in male dominated society. As widow she was taken as easy prey by males and it was difficult job to save herself from these vultures. She put up strong face and after initial problems she came out as a strong woman. When getting her became impossible then, group of males spread rumour that she was having affair and that was reason not to marry again. She wondered as why a woman is thought of in particular way only. Didn't she had heart and a body which felt pain and self respect which got trampled. So the life continued. And then she met Nafeesa. Two bonded like sisters or may be more than that. Pain had met pain. Their time used to pass in each other's company discussing about their lives. The dam had broken and emotions had flooded out. Nafeesa at times failed to decide that whose agony was more. One thing she was sure. Animal in man see no religion. It appears everywhere.

Anwar got commissioned in army and came home in uniform and seek blessings of his mother. When he came home, Nafeesa was not there. Enquiring, he reached house of Nahid to find his beloved mother. His heart came to mouth when he saw his mother bitterly crying as also Nahid. He was full of rage when he asked his mother who was reason of tears in her eyes. She avoided answer. Nahid couldn't. He came to know each and everything what had happened to his mother. He was full of hatred for his father. And then he came to know everything about Nahid too from Nafeesa. Nafeesa told him to forgive his father as it was different times. He asked a simple question "Can you forgive him?" Nafeesa was speechless. Nahid held her closely to allow her to cry.

Nafeesa liked Anjum who was now in college. She was ordinary looking girl but was full of respect and mannerism. Anwar was very good looking and Anjum was no match to him. For that reason Nafeesa didn't say anything to him though she confided with Nahid that she would have liked the relation. One day, Drabu came home very happy. Nafeesa had never asked him anything and in fact she had made it a habit to only answer in minimum words whatever was asked. He himself told her that minister Hayyat Khan had asked about marriage of Anwar with his daughter who was a very good looking girl. She didn't say anything. Telegram was sent to ask Anwar to come home. He was posted in Karachi and came within two days with worried looks about her. When Anwar was told about the proposal he was also happy.

Next day, when Nafeesa had gone to residence of Nahid, as was daily routine for her, Anwar went there to take Nafeesa for shopping. It was there he overheard Nafeesa and Nahid talking about him and he came to know that her mother wanted him to marry Anjum. Ordinary looking Anjum suddenly became extraordinary in his eyes as she was choice of his mother. Back home he waited for Nafeesa to come back. He then called his parents together to announce that he was interested in marrying Anjum and not daughter of minister. Drabu shouted and cried and pleaded but Anwar had no regard and concern for him. For him, decision had been taken by the person who mattered. Nafeesa had tears in her eyes. How can a son be so sacrificing? She had a son who had treated her as God whose decision was final. She couldn't sacrifice happiness of Anwar because of her desire do she pleaded with him to change decision but Anwar remained rock solid on his decision and had simple marriage with Anjum who came to his household as fragrance from fresh flowers. Drabu didn't like to see the face of Anjum, but couldn't do anything.

Anwar was blessed with a son after 3 years. She went to stay with Anjum in Rawalpindi where Anwar was posted as Major in Army. She remained there for about 3 months. For the first time, she had travelled out of Mirpur. Anwar insisted upon her to not go back and live with him only but, she had to go as Drabu had fallen sick and had nobody to look after. So, Anwar came to drop her back as her word was command for him. It was winter time and water of dam had receeded. It was time when old Mirpur would come out of water though in dilapidated condition. She asked Anwar to take her to old city. She was going there for first time after 50 years.

Reaching old city, she saw ruins of her Haveli. She could still see Haveli and it's verandah where, her father and brothers were butchered by Drabu. She fell down on verandah and was lifted by Anwar and Nahid who were accompanying her. She the place to Anwar where his grandfather and uncles were killed. She put soil of age on her head which was repeated by Anwar. She then went to ruins of Shiv Temple where miscreants had written offensive things on Temple walls. There was no idol there now, but she sat in prayer while, Anwar and Nahid waited out. Her life had come full circle.

❐

4
Megha And Family

Megha and Sudhir were happily married for five years and were blessed with a beautiful baby girl, Rati; two and half years after their marriage. Doting parents, as they both were, Rati was the apple of their eye. After Rati came into her life, Megha discontinued with her job as an Engineer in a big multinational construction house, to nurture Rati with her motherly care and affection. Her life totally revolved around her toddling daughter whom she groomed in the warmth of her bosom. Finances of the family got jolted; Sudhir, being the only earning hand, with an additional responsibility to cater. Nonetheless, the twosome felt blessed as Rati elated their lives by laying her footsteps in their highly mechanical lifestyle. The tiny yawn of his daughter, vanished Sudhir's fatigue of a frantic day at his workplace, the little hands touched their lives with immense joy and her innocent giggles rejuvenated their tiring days.

One Friday, the dark clouds of bad luck dawned upon Megha's small happy family, when she saw a stream of blood slobbering from Rati's mouth. Megha shook in her shoes as she saw the little one dazed at the sight of a bloody fluid pouring out of her mouth. Panic-struck, as she was, Megha rushed to the doctor right away. On way to hospital she gave call to Sudhir and was constantly sobbing. She couldn't utter a word but Sudhir could understand that something serious had happened. His first thought was that may be there was some accident. Finding Megha in no position to communicate with details, he asked. "Where are you?" Megha could muster all her strength and courage and regained her composer for few moments to feebly say "Rush to city hospital. Rati is in trouble." She hanged her mobile. Sudhir felt as if life had been drained out of him. He reached hospital in no times and took stairs to third floor Intensive Care Unit as he couldn't even wait for lift to arrive. He reached third floor running and totally breathless. Sight of blood stained frock of Rati created intense shooting pain in his chest and he felt like something has squeezed his heart and took all blood out of him.

The month that followed, was filled with days of fright and nights that lacked sleep as they kept switching between Jammu and Delhi for a thorough health check of their dear child. Sitting outside PET scan room and watching her little angel going inside Clusterphobic machine from glass window of moniter room sitting along with her childhood friend Dr. Vandana who was a renowned Radiologist now, she looked at moniter with fingers crossed at the phenomenon of labortary-created primodic anti matter colliding with body cells and leaving traces of disease fault line. she however could see her fate from the worried looks and sweating on the forehead of Dr. Vandan. A month later, the doctors broke the most scandalising news to the battling parents. Rati suffered from an advanced stage of blood cancer! Megha and Sudhir were taken back on their heels on the announcement of such horrifying information. The whole world had doomed for the parents of the afflicted daughter. It seemed as if their blissful life was suddenly evil struck, some wicked powers had casted misfortune on their contented family.

An emotional catastrophe hit Sudhir, who spent his sleepless nights looking vacantly at the ceiling of his dimly lit room, with a chain of thoughts dancing in his mind.

Megha, on the contrary, was a mentally strong woman who was able to take hold of her life even when life seemed to have come to an end. As Sudhir gave up on life in despair, Megha did not lose faith in God and in the mother in her. She battled back to save her daughter's life which seemed to be slipping away from her hands. She had to fight for her daughter, a fight which had been thrust upon her by God to test her patience and resolve.

As the doctors informed, Rati's disease had no perennial solution except for a regular body blood transfusion after every six months, a glimmer of hope arouse in the parents for Rati's survival. However, in spite of undergoing regular blood transfusion in the succeeding year, Rati's health deteriorated. Doctors, who gave up on the health condition of the ailing child, referred the patient to top cancer institute in Bangaluru, a hub of research work on new treatments for cancer.

Doctor Nanda, the top oncologist of Bangaluru, sow the seeds of hope in the minds of the troubled couple when she announced the possibility of a permanent treatment through placenta stem cell therapy, which required the use of placenta of the patient. Unfortunately, the placenta of the patient was not preserved in the stem cell bank during her birth. The sole solution left with the parents was to plan another baby, the placenta of which could be used to treat Rati permanently from the dreaded disease. The bargain was not as easy as it appeared on the papers, as Megha was reminded of the complications she had to undergo during her first pregnancy. The dialogue of her gynaecologist, "Don't conceive another baby ever. It will be a serious threat to your life." Hovered in her mind as she tried to cope with the unbelievable ramifications. She had been suffering from pre-eclampsia which could raise her blood pressure to such level that she couldn't survive during her delivery.

As the couple pondered over the matter, it was a tough call for Sudhir to choose between the devil and the deep sea.

"We cant fight with our destiny. We are making all efforts to save Rati but I won't allow you to put your life at stake and THAT'S FINAL." But for a mother, there couldn't have been an easier choice to make. Putting her life at stake so her daughter could live, was the most unchallenging option for her to take. Doctors intimated her about the risks that were involved in the decision that she had opted at a young age of 30. After vehement resistance from her husband, the wife chose the mother in her and decided to drink the bitter cup of suffering for the sake of her daughter's life. When all the pleadings failed to yield desired result in consonance with her resolve, she took Sudhir head on the hard way. "If something happened to Rati then I won't live too and will commit suicide." With heavy heart Sudhir succumbed to her decision as he was left with no choice. After two months as she broke the news of conception of a second baby, Sudhir broke down in tears as the approaching end of his wife haunted him. He left his job as a banker and decided to run his consultancy from home so as to accompany Megha in her battle of survival of three souls. He begged, he prayed, he craved for survival of his wife and his daughter both in front of the supremepower each day. His heart pounded faster each day as the date of delivery approached nearer. Finally, as the day of delivery arrived; a surreal smile came over the mother's face as she drew closer to her final stage of her battle, to commence a new beginning. As Megha was always inclined to look at the rosier side of the picture, she headed towards the operation theatre expecting a light at the end of the tunnel. She hoped to come back to her blissful abode she had reared with her blood and sweat. She kissed on Rati's hands as she neared the operation theatre and looked straight in the eyes of her husband, hoping to see him soon after the delivery. Sudhir poised to be calm in front of his five-year-old daughter and comforted her by assuring that her mother will be back soon. He kissed Megha on her forehead and said. "Don't worry. All will be well. God will be with you. Come soon healthy."

A few hours later, he kissed his wife's ice cold cheeks and forehead, the surreal smile on her face remained! He kept staring at her as he reminisced the most cherished moments with her, when he saw her for the first time, when he decided to stay with her for the lifetime, when he first held her in his arms, when he handed over Rati to her for the first time, when life was full of life! His lips quivered and tears began to roll down his cheeks as he regretted the times he had shouted at her in anger, the moments they had wasted fighting with each other, the chances he had missed to tell her how much he loved her, the occasions he had complained about the food she served and the services she rendered out of her devotion for him. Lost in the fond memories of his wife, Rati's convulsive gasps brought him back to where he was, in front of his dead wife!

Rati was given the appropriate treatment for chronic malignancy, thereafter. She loitered in every corner of Megha Niwas with her toddling brother crawling after her elder sister. Sudhir wrapped both his children in a cotton wool as if they were his precious jewels. His days were filled with the tunes of nursery rhymes, the imaginative storytelling, playing with the barbies and miniature cars, shopping of baby clothes, food and diapers and an hour of narrating them the tales of their mother each day. Megha's home, the name plate of which read, 'MEGHA AND FAMILY', was illuminated once again as the roars of laughter, noisy fights, naughty giggles and the ecstatic cries of the two kids echoed all over the house, with their mother casting a blissful eye upon her pearls from the heavens above.

❐

5
Choti Maa

When Swati came to her matrimonial home after marriage, she was welcomed by her elder sister-in-law Rohini with open arms and from the very first hug, a chemistry developed between the two. They were more than sisters. Rohini took care of Swati as a mother and never allowed Swati to feel as younger daughter-in-law of the house. She always pushed Swati ahead in prominence whenever occasion came. Rohini was Di to her she had always missed. Rohini was looking after household after death of her parents-in-law in accident and now had helping hand with Swati but she always saw child in Swati and never put her to tedious tasks and rather kept her to ease.

Rohini apparently was living a happy and contended life and with her helping nature and sweet manners was liked by all. Swati however could feel the hurt and pain behind happy looks of Rohini, the pain of not getting joy of motherhood even after seven years of marriage. When Swati got pregnant she shared desire with her husband Mohan of giving their first child in adoption to Rohini Di to giving meaning to her life too. Mohan had always been dutiful younger brother to his elder brother Saket and happily agreed and rather developed extreme respect for Swati for her sacrifice for the sake of family and elders. When boy was born to Swati, he was given in adoption to Rohini and Saket. Child was named Ashwin and brought joy and happiness to the life of Rohini and Saket. Ashwin was prince of the house and was apple to the eyes of Rohini who was ever thankful and grateful to Swati for her decision.

Time passed and Saket got promoted in his bank as manager and posted in Kanpur. Mohan felt happy for the promotion but was upset as he had to live without his brother and Bhabhi and also Ashwin. But they could do nothing as they had taken decision on life of Ashwin and was satisfied that Ashwin will get better life with Rohini and Saket who were financially better placed. So the unwanted separation happened.

Rohini and Saket came back to Delhi when Swati conceived second time and gave birth to a daughter Ananya but went back within a week as school of Ashwin was to open. Swati got busy in bringing up Ananya and almost forget about Ashwin except remain in touch with Rohini on phone once a day and also getting informed about Ashwin. When Ashwin was seven years old, a miracle of sought happened with Rohini conceiving. Swati was so happy for her and remained with Rohini for almost three months till she deliver her son Rohan.

As it would had been difficult for Rohini to take care of both children on her own, Saket tried for his transfer back to Delhi. He had in the meanwhile got promoted as general nanager and had made lot of money by means not always legal. He had to spend about five lakhs to get himself transferred back to Delhi. It was again reunion of families and in joint family it was rather easy for both ladies to manage three kids between them. Coming about one year of age, Rohan was so much attached to Swati that she forget herself being natural mother of Ashwin. For Swati Rohan was more important than her own two kids and Rohan also was always hanging around her. For him only person important was Choti Maa. As Rohini couldn't breast fed Rohan because of medical condition, Swati fed Rohan with her own milk. She at times ignored Ananya who was almost of same age as Rohan.

With passage of time, the relationship became more strong only. Swati was always worrying about Rohan and to some extent Ananya. Saket in the meanwhile had retired and started his own construction company and in comparatively less time his construction company became top company of the Delhi. Major contribution in the progress of company was from untiredly efforts by Ashwin who after completing his engineering has taken over as managing director of the company. Ashwin also addressed Swati as Choti Maa like Rohan. She never expressed openly but natural love and affection of mother was always there.

With passage of more time, Ashwin got married and Rohan and Ananya joined university. One day Rohini met with accident outside her house and died in arms of Swati on road after taking promise that Swati will always take care of her both sons. Swati for first time felt without support. She was used to always live under protective umbrella of Rohini. Mohan in the meanwhile fell sick and became bedridden. Ashwin was however taking care of everyone.

Saket had taken to drinking in a big way after death of Rohini. He developed lung cancer and despite best of treatment couldn't survive. Swati was the only elder member of family left in control as Mohan was in vegetable state only. After a week of death of Saket, his advocate came to the household to read his last will. Swati knew that Mohan would have divided his property equally amongst Ashwin and Rohan. She sat there with all family members for just formality. She was holding hand of Rohan who was sobbing over death of Saket. He was only left with his Choti Maa. Others didn't matter for him. When will was read over Swati was in for a big shock. Saket had given everything to Rohan including company and Ahmad just left a small shop for Ashwin which belonged to their grandfather. Swati felt sudden pain in her heart. Saket never considered Ashwin as his son and had only used him as employee. For Saket son was only Rohan. She felt extreme hatred for herself of having spoiled life of Ashwin for her idealism. She looked towards Ashwin to find him staring at her with tears in eyes. Her hand trembled and she left hand of Rohan, who was also under shock.

Will of Mohan did came as surprise to Rohan too as the whole business empire had been created by his elder brother Ashwin with his hard work. He however remained silent and left it to elders to decide on the issue. No will could change his relation with his family, that for sure he knew. But since that day behaviour of his Choti Maa changed towards him. Gone was the warmth of love and now it was more a formality. But he ignored. Swati on her own was feeling ashamed of her herself of what had happened to Ashwin because of her decision and this awakened the sleeping mother of Ashwin in her. She was now taking extra care and giving more attention to Ashwin, who though dejected and tense but continued looking after his work of company. Rohan executed attorney in favour of Ashwin to run the accounts of company and so things moved on. But Swati stood where she was left by reading of will stuck. Ashwin could now deal with company but as an agent of Rohan only. Rohan thought he had done his duty by surrendering all his powers to Ashwin and he never checked working and accounts of company. For him company belonged to Ashwin.

Behaviour of Rohan made his Choti Maa more upset and angry and she expected Rohan to rectify mistake of his father by surrendering half of assests to Ashwin but instead he had only given attorney. She could have withstood any humiliation and insult for herself but not injustice done to her first born particularly when she was herself to blame for the ordeal of Ashwin. An angry and humiliated mother can go to any extent to undo wrong to her child, this truth struck her in very hard way.

She tolerated everything for about a year and then her tolerance have way. She decided to take upon herself to undo harm to Ashwin. It was hot summers day of July when she laced lunch prepared for Rohan by her with poison. Rohan always took food which was prepared by his Choti Maa even when his mother was alive. By evening he was vomitting blood and was found in almost dead position by servant on his bed room. He was shifted to hospital by servant as Swati after serving lunch to Rohan had left home to avoid any suspicion to her after death of Rohan. She had replaced food with non-poisonous food after Rohan had taken food so that if police came and check food it would be found good. She took poisonous left over food and threw that in river.

In hospital, it took four days for Rohan to recover. It was easily detected by police that he was given poison in food when his stomach food residue was sent for laboratory and was waiting him. To make statement to indicate who had given poison to him and in what way as it was established in investigation that there was no reason for him to commit suicide. While other members of family were all eagerly waiting to know who had done crime, Swati was trembling with fear. She knew Rohan had understood everything and would inform police. She was not in position to prepare herself for humiliation and imprisonment.

When Inspector went to Rohan along with magistrate to take his statement after doctor declares him fit to make statement, everyone else was looking through the door while statement was being recorded. They couldn't hear what Rohan was saying but could see from facial expressions of Inspector and Magistrate that they were shocked and were asking questions to Rohan to know more. Swati got sweating all over her face and she felt extremely cold even in July. She felt like stone and couldn't move her limbs.

Inspector came out of room and everyone rushed to him to know the truth. Inspector took sometime before announcing that Rohan had taken Parshad from some religious person on road and may be that was poisonous as that religious person may be some criminal in disguise who wanted to kill Rohan to loot him. Stream of tears rolled down from eyes of Swati. She ran inside room and fell on Rohan sobbing heavily. Other members also came in. She couldn't beg forgiveness by words but her tears were crying loud. She folded her hands to Rohan before leaving room. Repeated calls of "Choti Maa" from Rohan couldn't stop her.

Same evening dead body of Swati was found inside her car which had met with accident with a truck. Police was still baffled about car going on extreme wrong side and colliding with truck. May be she was disturbed because of almost death of her favourite son. Rohan was shattered while he lit pyre of his Choti Maa. He was deprived of love of mother who always loved him more than his own mother, notwithstanding her attempt to kill him. Everything stood clear to him. His own father was to be blamed for everything happening.

After fourteenth day of Choti Maa, Rohan executed documents and shifted all property in name of Ashwin. He repented that he had not done this earlier otherwise Choti Maa would have been alive.

❐

6
Debt

It was first day of entering temple of justice for young Antriksh. He had recently passed out from Law College and taken license of advocate. He had high hopes and ambitions months Profession. He went to leading advocate of state with his bio data containing certificate of brilliant academic achievements and his participation certificates on moot courts at national level. He thought that he would be welcomed by any law firm or senior and was shocked to hear no from senior advocate to whom he had gone for apprenticeship citing excuse of no possibility of taking new assistant in view of number of junior advocates already with him. Antriksh could understand situation. He then moved to almost all leading law firms but answer from all were same. To his utter dismay, he found lot many of his juniors joining good offices, just because they had influence and connections.

After about two months of efforts to join established law firm, he came at face with reality. He had to start on his own. How could he succeed in a highly competitive profession with no godfather or senior and with neither professional training nor client-age. Choice was less and he had no time to waste. That day he resolved to fight on his own to earn his place in profession. His past life moved across field of his mind. He could see himself, an orphan, selling newspaper and then studying in govt. school. Then to selling milk and starting his poultry farm. He never begged for any favour from anyone, not even god. Whatever he had got in his life was only on hardwork and untiring efforts.

Antriksh however got dejected as litigants were not willing to bet on him with no professional training and experience. He however continued his efforts and started drafting cases for other advocates on paltry amounts to sustain himself. On briefs prepared by him, many lawyers were arguing cases. He had satisfaction, though not name. Then he was called by Senior Advocate Ashok Sharma who because of advance age was not in position to continue in profession. He asked Antriksh to sit in his office and handle all his briefs. Life had changed for Antriksh. Finally, his patience was rewarded and now he had office as also fairly large number of cases. He never looked back and in few years he made his name in courts. Judges were also impressed by his advocacy skills and oratory command despite his educational background of govt. school.

One day when he was sitting in high court waiting for his case to be called, he was called by bench. He was told that a convict and written letter of appeal to Chief Justice against his conviction in a murder case wherein he had been sentenced to death penalty. Antriksh was asked by court to appear for convict as amicus on payment of nominal fee by legal aid. He had never done any murder case before but couldn't say no to honour bestowed upon him. He accepted the offer and copy of case paper-book was provided to him.

Antriksh went back home and for next one week he was reading file to prepare arguments but was clueless as the case was proved by dying declaration of an eye witness who had seen the murder himself but while crossing road to reach victim was hit by a speeding vehicle which resulted in his death but not before he made statement to magistrate about murder. Antriksh went to jail to meet his client and ask him about case and also to get his Attorney signed. Inside jail he was taken to waiting area from where he could see the inside compound of jail where a young person was giving training of martial art to jail inmates. Warden asked him to sit and wait for Guruji. That was first meeting with his client Keshav who was known as Guruji for fellow jail inmates. Keshav came and sat down on floor besides him. Antriksh had many questions but Keshav refused to answer any of them. Antriksh was annoyed "If you didn't want your case to be argued then why had you written letter to Chief Justice." He got no reply to even this and then Keshav left after signing Attorney. He could see calmness and pain on the face of Keshav.

Next week case got listed. Antriksh went to court but was clueless in the arguments despite his all efforts. When case was called and he stood up to dias to start his arguments he was interrupted by senior judge on the bench by saying there was nothing in case in favour of convict and that he had been engaged as of formality to give right of defence to accused. He then could understand the behaviour of Keshav. He was also angry with the judges to have used him for formality. Something changed in him and he resolved to give his best shot to the case. He asked for adjournment of case to prepare it thoroughly which was given by judges with smile. He felt insulted by that smile.

Case was taken for hearing after a month. This time he was ready. He put out his main plea. Dying declaration of eye witness was not admissible and couldn't be used against Keshav as dying declaration is relevant only to the circumstances leading to own death of its maker and not about death of someone else. That was brilliant move.

Judges were also taken by surprise and he got what seemed impossible a month ago, verdict of acquittal for Keshav. He had won not only his first major case but judges also praised him in the judgment.

After three days, he opened door of his early morning on ringing of call bell and found Keshav standing on door with Parsad. Keshav had gone to Vaishno Devi Temple after he was realised from jail and was coming direct from there to Antriksh. Antriksh was living alone in the small house he had taken on rent. Keshav came in and Antriksh prepared tea for him. After he had taken tea, he was still sitting on sofa. Antriksh was getting late for court so he told Keshav to go now as he was free. "You have saved me from certain death. Now this life is yours. I won't go anywhere", said Keshav. Antriksh was taken aback. He was not prepared to have Keshav in his life but Keshav ignored all his logic. Antriksh told Keshav to leave in angered voice and went to court after locking door and leaving Keshav on roadside. When he came back in evening he saw Keshav sleeping near his door. He woke him and took him in and gave food. He now understood that there was no way to avoid Keshav. From that day Keshav became his shadow. He was clerk, munshi, driver, cook, etc. of Antriksh.

After about a year thereafter Antriksh got married to Sunanda and by thus time Antriksh was well established as advocate. He arranged for a job for Keshav as bouncer in a club of his client in Delhi. It took Antriksh lot if efforts and finally swearing to make Keshav to go to Delhi to join job. At railway station Keshav was inconsolable but had no choice in view of swearing by Antriksh.

In five years time life had changed significantly. Antriksh had shifted to bigger house and was blessed with a daughter Somaya and a son Aakarshan, both were twins.

It was early morning in the winters of January that there was someone at the door pressing call bell. Antriksh went to open the door and there he was Keshav again with his luggage. He had come back after leaving his job. Keshav told him that he had left job of club two years back and then he joined as bodyguard of a leading film actor but was missing peace of mind and so he had left job and came to his saviour. There was hardly any choice, so Keshav started living with them as family member. He was helping hand to Sunanda and took extra care of both kids. He became Keshu

Chacha of both kids and then to all kids of locality. He never asked for anything except food. Antriksh however always brought things for Keshav what he purchased for himself. Keshav became Rakhi Bhai of Sunanda.

Time flew past and in this time Antriksh grew high in stature and had little time for family but Keshav was always there to take care of whole family. He was bodyguard of both kids particularly Somaya who had entered college. When Somaya was harassed by students in the name of ragging, she informed not her parents but Keshu Chacha and next day all persons who harassed her were begging pardon from her. Antriksh by thus time had become top criminal lawyer of the state and had number of enemies also including gangsters against who he was appearing as advocate. He never had fear of anyone.

It was on 24th May that Aakarshan was kidnapped by a gang and asked for ransom. Antriksh had no option than to pay hefty amount as ransom but shockingly even after getting ransom the gang refused to release Aakashan. Matter was then reported to police but nothing was forthcoming.

It was over a week since Aakarshan was kidnapped and there was no clue about him. Sunanda and Somaya had not taken food for almost complete week and were always crying, looking at door for Aakarshan to come which never happened. Antriksh had almost gone mad for his child. It was then Somaya went to her Keshu Chacha "Only you can bring him back. Please do something Chachu." Keshav looked at Antriksh who also had pleadings only in his eyes of helpless father craving to meet his son. Keshav nodded and went out.

In next one week it was not Keshav but Guruji who had come alive and revived his old contacts with criminals. News and information travel much faster in crime world than police network. One evening he got information from his source of the place where Aakarshan was kept. His gang was prepared for rescue mission, though it was frought with dangers.

Next morning Aakarshan came home unharmed, though in bad condition and Keshav was taken to hospital with his three friends and nine kidnappers. All brought dead. Probably, the most gruesome gang war. Also reused were 14 kids who were kidnapped from different places and kept in hideout by kidnappers. Joy and happiness of Antriksh and family was short lived when Aakarshan told them about Keshav. All rushed to hospital but it was too late. Bullet had hit Keshav on chest and torn through his heart golden heart. Antriksh was in shock and had to be injected sedatives and so was Somaya. Keshav had paid his debt through his blood and life. Keshav never dies. He lives in the hearts of his family. Antriksh got a letter from suitcase of Keshav written to him but never posted where he had narrated the murder Keshav committed, of person who had kidnapped his wife and killed her after ravishing her modesty.

Antriksh knew nothing how to pay back Debt of Keshav. May be in next birth, if there is one.

❐

7
Unspoken Friendship

It was first day of university and customary introductory party was going on. Every fresher was being asked a specific task beside his introduction. Arvind had already sung song, Fidda had delivered dialogues of movies and Roshan had read his own poem. Prakash was getting mentally prepared to play his part but was having no idea what task will be put to him. All freshers were competing for trophy of Best Fresh Student where maximum marks were reserved for performance in task completion. So far Roshan was way ahead. He also must had scored in looks, confidence and positive thinking beside his schooling from top boarding school.

When his turn came Prakash was given task to narrate true life event which should be moving and with life values. That was most difficult job. His life had seen so many ups and downs that it was difficult to decide in few minutes which incident to narrate but when he closed his eyes, the answer immediately flashed across board of his mind Ashraf. So he started narrating life incident which was laced with overtone of emotions, failure and lesson.

Prakash thus narrated: When I entered we were group of three close friends who moved together except for one period when one of us Savarkar had to go to other class for opted different subject. Life was without hassles and carefree. None of us was too good in studies but none was bothered about future, the life had in store for us. We left it our destiny to decide for us.

Within a year in college, Savarkar got selected for Engineering course and left state. Friendship and communication remained but distance had its impact. So now it was group of two persons – me and Raj. Together always and all situations and events. I used to go to college in public transport Matador while Raj was living just closed to college.

It was there I saw Ashraf for first time. He was also taking Matador from same stop as me. He was in our class, though section and classroom was different. I was captain of college wrestling team and he also came in trials, though he couldn't get selected. It started with slight nod of head by him and reciprocation by me in similar fashion. It didn't go beyond this.

Ashraf was smart and thorough gentleman and good at studies. He always moved alone and had no friend in college. He had recently shifted to Jammu from Doda and had not many persons known. I discussed with Raj and we decided to make friendship with him as we found warmth in his smile and greetings when he started wishing us both and we reciprocated, though there was no word spoken and it was restricted to smiles and nodding of heads only.

Many time I thought of talking to him at Matador stand or in Matador but somehow there was some hesitation which stopped me. I could see same hesitation in his eyes and in fact Raj was also having same delima. Time passed and we remained where we were. Our minds and hearts had accepted friendship but acknowledgment by words and deeds was pending. Then exam time came and Raj and me used to prepare for exams together, either he staying at my place or vice versa.

One day we were preparing perhaps science paper when we couldn't understand a problem. It was evening time. Raj said we should ask from Ashraf who would know answer for sure. We searched for his telephone number from college directory and I called. Call was picked by probably his mother. After wishing her I asked whether I could talk to Ashraf. She asked my number and told that he will call back.

We got his call after an hour and he asked for excusing him as he was busy in rituals of his father as it was 40th day of death of his father. It was such a shock. We were speechless. I asked him forgiveness as we didn't know that and told him we both would come to him. He said there was no need to come and said we could come after exams would be over. We couldn't muster courage to ask him our problem.

We decided to go to him after exams and add him to our group and to remain with him for rest of our life. But destiny had other plans. It was last day of exams. I was at Matador stand waiting for vehicle when I saw him coming from other side. He was totally shaken and seemed lost. I waited for him to cross road so that I could offer my condolences and to hug him.

But things didn't happen the way I was visuling. My dream was shaken by screahing noise of brakes being applied and then loud scream of Ashraf. He had been hit by a goods carrier and was lying in pool of blood on road. I rushed to him and took his head in my lap with his blood all over my clothes. He looked straight in my eyes with friendship, the unspoken words we three were waiting to speak. I was trebling and was feeling goosebumps because of fear and anxiety. That moment I opened my mouth to speak to my friend and assure him nothing will happen to him and that we will live together as friends ever. I looked in his eyes to start speaking. But there was no light and he was not blinking eyes. He had gone even before I could speak a word. Our friendship remained silent. Not a word spoken, though acknowledgment was always there.

Never again I waited to acknowledge relation or feeling with anyone in life. Lesson Ashraf taught me got imprinted in my soul. Never put to tomorrow what should be done today. Tomorrow never comes.

Prakash ended his story thus. Not a single applause but with around 80 pairs of moist eyes, some crying loud some weeping some shaken but all moved. He lifted trophy of Best Fresher that year for his friend Ashraf.

❐

8
Umbilical Cord

Aishwarya was the youngest daughter after her two brothers and was the princess of the house and apple of the eyes of her father who was serving as Colonel in the army. Whatever she said was mostly honoured by her parents and brothers. By the time she entered Engineering college, her both elder brothers were married and eldest brother Vinod who was Inspector in police was blessed with son. Sending Aishwarya to hostel in different city was a difficult decision for the family but her career was more important and so she came to Delhi to study engineering course in one of top colleges of the country.

As her hostel was near college and was at walking distance only she never needed vehicle except when she had to go to market. There was an auto-rickshaw stand outside her hostel so she and her roommate Kavita fixed with one auto-rickshaw driver Anik to carry them to market whenever they had to go out. Anik was a young person with good looks and attractive mannerism and knew art of speaking sweetly, and he used his skills in abundance. He had studied only up to higher secondary but with his communication skills he could make friend easily.

With passing of time, Aishwarya became very comfortable with Anik and before she could restrain or control herself, she was head over heels in love with Anik who had sown seeds of love in her impressionable mind with uncanny skills. She understood the meaning of such relationship and what effect it would bring to her life and family but she was really helpless or so she thought. Anik made his moves with skill of chess player and bringing physicality to relation was part of his strategy to leave no choice for Aishwarya. Once she took that step it became impossible for her to retract.

When Aishwarya told her family about decision to marry Anik, Col. Mehta fell down on floor and had to be lifted and taken to doctor. What followed was a very long battle between former princess and the wronged family. Words of her father never left ringing in her ears for rest of her life. "You will be reason for death of your father physically though you have already killed him with your decision." To equal effect were words of her mother. "You will never live in peace after bringing disrepute to your family." It was only later on she realised how correct her parents were.

She did marry Anik in court and then Arya Samaj. Her brothers tried to stop marriage by threatening Anik but failed because of stand taken by Aishwarya. Love is blind after all. She went to her matrimonial house and soon realised that actual life is entirely different from love talks of persons in courtship. For few months initially only Anik was good to her and then he started showing his true colours. She had in the meanwhile joined govt. job and Anik had also got himself registered as Class C contractor and was taking small contracts with Municipality. The problem started with Anik forcing her to leave job but she plainly refused as that was her only solace as there was no person with whom she could share her grief. Anik had forcibly stopped her from talking to even her friends and had taken her mobile too.

Within one year of marriage Anik started forcing her to conceive but she was not prepared as she was not sure about her own future. She had already started repenting on not listening to better advice of her family but Anik the master player knew that once she becomes mother all her options would be closed, the same method he used before marriage. So he became very good to her and made her agree for child which would cement their relations. She again got be fooled and so she became mother. Sanjeev came as bundle of joy in her life. The only good thing which had happened to her in long time. She forgot all her problems with Sanjeev with her.

With passing of time, the tortures of Anik became more intense and by now he had started not only abusing but beating Aishwarya also. He told her that he had been insulted by her father and brother and thus was revenge for that. Hearing such insulting words after such long period of marriage came as a shock. When she could tolerate no more she decided to walk out and told Anik that she was leaving him and would take Sanjeev with her. Before she could move out her mother-in-law took Sanjeev forcibly to their native village and didn't even allow Aishwarya to meet him for more than two months. She left matrimonial home and shifted to hostel totally broken. One night she thought of committing suicide by jumping in Yamuna and in fact went to bridge but left idea at last moment and decided to fight for her son. Being ashamed of what she had done to her family she had no courage to go to them for help and neither she felt any right over them but her guilt was killing her and unless her family pardon her it was difficult to live in peace. She picked her mobile and sent message to her father "I got punishment for not listening to you. Sorry for being reason of all troubles in your life. In next I would like to again your daughter and live life according to you".

Next day afternoon she was weeping and crying on the shoulder of her mother with her father holding her hands and her brothers and their wives standing along in her hostel room. She had not lost everything. Her family was still there. Umbilical cord was not broken. Her father said the kind words: "You continue to be our princess. We suffered more than you with you not around."

She came back home and after six months started fight for getting her son back. It was very exhausting effort and after long drawn court litigation she finally got custody of her son back. The day Sanjeev came to her parental home all eyes were wet with the scene of mother meeting son after nine months and rest of family meeting Sanjeev for first time. Through tears she washed away all her sorrows and tortuous memories. She had now reason to live, her bundle of joy and she had strength to fight, the strength of her family standing with her.

She saw her son growing and inculcated good principles and morality in him so that he can treat everyone with love and care and that he should have respect for human feelings, to live in peace and mutual respect. She wondered how many girls get second chance like she got because of her parents and brothers.

❒

9
Bilqees

Bilqees was getting married to Mohammad Mir who was 32 years elder to her at 51 years, even elder by four years to her father Yaqoob. In fact, Yaqoob was deep in debt and life had become difficult for family of Yaqoob to sustain with one pair earning hands in family of seven. That was one he decided to get her daughter married to richest person of village Mohammad Mir who had promised to take care of all financial problems of family. Bilqees had one elderly daughter Rafia but Mohammad Mir chose her as she was way more beautiful than Rafia. So she was asked by father to prepare for her sacrifice, of getting married to a person who was more than age of her father and who, as per rumours, had burnt alive his first wife on minor fight. She always wanted to marry her cousin Rashid who was two years elder to him. They loved each other and had exchanged promise of marriage. But fate is cruel and so is life. When life ask for sacrifice, it takes away the very best one have.

She came to house of Mohammad Mir after marriage and soon realised that rumours about him were not false. Mohammad Mir was person of very high temper and used to get agitated on trival issues and then followed abuses, torture, and beatings. She forgot even the counts how many time she was thrown out of house and how many shivering nights she had to spend outside door in winters in Kupwara.

Her husband even had no concern to at least throw a blanket at her. But he had kept his promise. All debts of Yaqoob were clear and he was running a shop gifted by his soninlaw and economically family was secured, insecurities of Bilqees apart.

It was peak of militancy and during night there was always curfew. She saw number of strangers coming to her husband at odd hours and she was on strict instructions during those time to remain in her room and bolt from inside. Then series of arrests started in village and number of persons were killed in encounter. The number was alarming. It was one chilly night that her husband was picked by army and taken out. After sometimes there was firing but nobody dared to go out during night. In the morning, villagers saw trail of blood near Jehlum stream and signs of dragging dead body. What had happened last night was very obvious. The dead body must have reached Pakistan-occupied Kashmir by that time. There was lot of crying and weeping. Militants also came to her house proclaiming her husband to be Amir of Hizb but she was not concerned. There were no tears in her eyes and why should there be even one with the cruelties inflicted upon her. She came back to her parental home but not before her father got all properties of Mohammad Mir transferred in her name. She was treated as Queen in house.

She met Rashid again after six years. He was working in forest department as Guard. From her mother she came to know Rashid had refused to marry as he loved some girl who was no more but reality was known to her only besides Rashid. May be Allah had given her second lease of life. In about five months, she was married to Rashid with stars in her eyes.

Life with Rashid was all bliss. He was so caring and loving that Bilqees forgot all pains inflicted by Mohammad Mir very soon. In next five years she became mother of two sons and one daughter. All her sisters were also married except youngest one who was studying in MBBS in Govt Medical College Srinagar. She was always thanking Allah for bringing her to Heavens after showing her hell.

Then everything changed one day. There was big meeting called by militants to introduce to people their new Divisional Commander. It was huge gathering and then Divisional Commander came.... Mohammad Mir with mark of bullet on his half face and left arm dangling like lifeless. He was telling public how he was thrown in river presumed dead and how he reached Pakistan and recovered in hospital after long treatment. He then joined trying camp in Mirpur and was then sent to Afghanistan with Talibans. He had come back to his people to fight for Azadi.

Bilqees having married to someone else and having children which she couldn't bear from him was just intolerable to Divisional Commander of Hizb-ul-Muzahidin. He summoned Rashid to surrender Bilqees to him and keep children as Bilqees continued to be wife of Mohammad Mir only as per Shariah laws. Rashid was in no position to say no but Bilqees could muster courage to say no. How can she be compelled to leave Rashid and live with monster Mohammad Mir who always treated her with extreme cruelty and how on earth can someone ask a mother to live without minor children. Unfortunately, her father also was on side of her enemy, whatever may be reason.

To give legitimacy to whole issue, Mohammad Mir called meeting of village headman and Molvi to give verdict which was on expected line. It said though marriage of Bilqees with Rashid is not Haram as she married when her husband was presumed dead and her children are also legitimate but as her first husband is still alive and alone has got right over her person so she had to move to Mohammad Mir leaving children to Rashid who can marry younger sister of Bilqees to take care of children. Next Friday was fixed day of Rukhsati when Bilqees would move to house of Mohammad Mir. It was already Thursday. That night she slept with Rashid and all three kids in same bed hugging them tightly. She had additional problem of life of her younger sister also put on stakes along with lives of her husband and kids, least to say her own. That was difficult and longest night of her life.

In the morning relatives of Mohammad Mir came to take Bilqees. They took Bilqees but she was ice cold, lifeless. They also took bottle of rat poison which was found in her hand in morning.

❐

10
Maryada

When Maryada was in hostel in Dehradoon, she always missed home. During summer vacations also she hardly had opportunity to go back to home as her mother Vinita used to take her from hostel and then two of them used to be on long tours, sometimes within country but mostly out of country to exotic places for whole of vacations and then she used to go back to hostel. In between she got opportunity to visit her home, a really palatial place and meet her family consisting of her father and long army of cousins and uncles and aunts. Her interactions with her father Kumar were very cordial and full of care and love. Kumar used to visit her almost every month in hostel. She lived life of luxury but was always perplexed why she alone was in hostel whereas all her cousins were staying home. However, she had occasions and opportunities to visit the very best locations of the world. One thing which always disturbed her was the coldness and non-responsiveness in relationship of her parents. She had never seen them happy together.

She was completing her higher school and her stay in boarding would be finally over in about a month's time. She was always immersed in thought of going back and living with her family and enjoying normal life, though she would miss freedom and liberty and her friends particularly Priya who had been her bestfriend since the day she entered boarding school. They shared all their secrets and thoughts and were like one soul in two bodies.

Coming back home was a real shocker for her within first few days when she saw that her parents were not sharing bedroom and were in fact living separately under the same roof. She could be face on with reality that her parents were not even on talking terms and on enquiry she was told that things were like this for years. She was grown up girl of 18 years of age and could understand what was happening around. She got admission in local medical college in undergraduate course but decided not to stay in hostel to bridge gap between her parents as she loved both of them.

It's difficult to hide truth with so many eyes and ears around. Her cousin Neeraj who was of her age revealed everything to her, about his father mercilessly beating her mother for trival issues and non-issues and her mother being given medical treatment on number of occasions, about drinking habit of her father which was root cause of all problems, about company of bad people with her father which had lot of influence on him.

She decided to rebuilt relationship of her parents brick by brick and her efforts did have some effect but only Kumar was In senses. After evenings Kumar used to be entirely different personality having no regards or respect for anyone and least of them to Vanita whom he abused and blamed for everything which had gone wrong to him in life.

Maryada was a brilliant student in her boarding school but her performance in medical college was below average because of constant torture and mental pressure she was undergoing. There was no Priya also who could share her traumas and tensions. Life was a complete mess but her priority was her parents and studies was taking back seat as she had no time to regain her composer and calm.

It was chilly winter of January when she came home from her college library and heard noise even outside her residence. Taking long stride she rushed inside to find her cousins and other family members standing in open area while sounds of shouting and crying was coming from bedroom of her father. Nobody dared to enter his room. Her uncle Ravi who was elder brother of her father told her to go in and save her mother as her father could only listen to her. She knew that her father loved her too much and would not dare say no to her. She rushed towards bedroom.

In the bedroom, the scene was horrific. Kumar was dead drunk and was having his leather belt in his hands while Vinita was lying on th floor with her dress torn and bruises all over body with blood coming out of side of head. She fell on her mother and shouted at Kumar. "Are you human or beast." Kumar was already seething with rage and anger and was heavily under influence of intoxicants. Word of hatred from Maryada pierced him deep inside. In for of rage he through the wooden stool lying near him on floor and left room shouting abuses.

Before Vinita could regroup herself, she saw stool thrown by Kumar hitting floor and then hitting Maryada on head. Then she remembered stream of blood coming from head of Maryada as she fell unconscious. She shouted loud "Maryada is injured." In next moment, Kumar came running in room and held Maryada in his arms. He was shocked to see that stool he had thrown on floor to show his anger had actually hit Maryada on head. Even in his drunken stage, he died multiple times looking at blood of his life Maryada.

Maryada was shifted to hospital immediately but was announced brought dead by doctors. When her dead body was handed over Kumar fell at the feet of Vinita who was neither concious nor unconscious, standing like stone. All her last rites were performed by her parents together. She succeeded in her death what she couldn't attain in life.

Kumar sold all her properties and opened school for orphans in the name of Maryada where he was now serving underprivileged students for charity. He also was now running a deaddiction centre Maryada so that no Maryada should die before her father could realise human relations and lessons of mutual respect. Vinita was working with him on both projects. Maryada lives.

❐

11
Mother-In-Law

Two small girls were playing in the ground all by themselves, unmindfull of happenings around. It was summertimes and it was really hot but they were enjoying their playing and their company together. They were friends since the day they went to school together in same class. And since that day they had become inseparable. Sarita and Neelam. School staff and class teachers also tried to separate them and to at least ensure they sit on different benches in class as together they were always creating trouble in class with their pranks. But they were both excellent in studies and first two positions in class in annual examination were always rotating between them. That was time when TV has not yet knocked at the doors of social relations and people had time for each other. In neighbourhood of Sarita someone had brought TV and every Sunday he used to allow whole Mohalla to watch movie on his TV in morning time. There used to be huge rush with hall fully packed and people especially kids of locality sitting on floor to watch movies on black and white television. They had also gone there on one or two occasions but didn't like idea of wasting time, even watching movies. They would rather prefer to study together or play.

They moved from school to college together but their friendship only grew stronger. They were inseparable. And then Sarita got engaged to Bhushan who was living in Amritsar. That was decision of family. She resisted and Neelam also pleaded for not sending Sarita away but boy was good as also family and so marriage took place and Sarita moved to Amritsar. The inseparable were separated. Life continued. Neelam joined university and kept herself busy. Sarita was blessed with a boy. More than anyone else Neelam was escatic. She went to Amritsar to meet her nephew with lot of gifts and stayed with Sarita for a week. She was treated like daughter in family and was so satisfied to see Sarita living happily with her husband and her bundle of joy whom she named Krishna. That was her right as Massi.

Neelam also got married thereafter with Satish who was a businessman running his finance company. She found in Satish a nice human being who cared for feelings of others. Sarita was with her during all marriage ceremonies along with Bhushan and Krishna. Cycle of life moved on and after two years Neelam was blessed with a beautiful girl named Sonakshi by Sarita. While family of Sarita was comparatively rich and there came some financial problems to Satish because of change in law for running financial companies but Neelam never discussed that with Sarita. When Sonakshi was 9 years old, Sarita fell sick and was admitted to hospital. It was found that her both kidneys have failed and chance of her survival was meek unless there can be kidney transplant from a healthy donar. Bhushan tested himself but there was no match so Sarita finally resiled to faith and start closing things and planning things which would take place after she would leave. She was majorly concerned about Krishna who was only 12 years old. She decided that Krishna will be given in custody to Neelam and got Satish agreed for this.

While she was admitted in PGI Chandigarh one day doctor told her that a voluntary donar has come whose parameters are also matching but he doesn't want his identity to be disclosed. She and Satish were so happy. She would get chance to see Krishna growing. Operation was successful but after operation Satish was spending less time with her and attending more the donar who was recovering in adjoining ward. She could know identity only after she fully recovered and went on wheelchair to meet donar Neelam.

Life cycle moved on. Sonakshi turned out to be a beautiful, polite and soft-spoken girl with very good manners. Sarita decided to ask Neelam for marriage of Krishana with Sonakshi, of course after asking Krishna and Bhushan. Neelam was reluctant because of financial disparities in two families but agreed as she had immense faith in Sarita and that Sonakshi will be happy with Sarita around. Marriage took place with pump and show.

There was one compatibility between Krishna and Sonakshi. Krishna was pampered and very loud and whenever he used to raise voice Sonakshi became terrified and start crying. They were fighting on small and trivalent issues but situation was becoming bad to worse. When Neelam heard this, she was in total shock. How can Sonakshi be unhappy or maltreated in house of her Sarita. She and Satish went to Amritsar and mediate and got things settled. Unthinkable happened. In rage, Krishna used abusing language against Sonakshi and Neelam both. When Satish scolded him of abusing Neelam who was like his mother, Bhushan interjected and said, "I know what type of woman Neelam is. Don't compel me to open my mouth". To her own horror, Sarita found her taking side of her son and husband and asked Neelam and Satish to leave her house immediately. Satish took weeping and crying Sonakshi also with him and Sarita didn't stop them and was staring like a stone.

There were efforts to patch up by relatives and Sonakshi came back two tickets,message but both times she went back. Sarita was more local with Sonakshi and she was fighting more with herself what she was doing to her daughter, to daughter of her friend Neelam who saved her life but situations always make her loss temper, though subsequently she had to repent to herself. It was last time, even when Neelam came alone to take Sonakshi back finally. She didn't say anything but asked for one-to-one meeting with Sarita for sake of old times. They met in Sarita's bedroom. Sitting outside of bed Sarita waited for Neelam to outburst and blast and she was preparing herself to match her. But Neelam was not saying anything. Then Neelam took Sarita's hand in her hands and said "Khush rehana" Sarita looked at her face. There was no anger or pain. It was totally emotionless and white as all blood from face had been taken out. That face haunted her for next one month, making her spend sleepless nights.

Sarita spent one month tormented what has been done to Neelam and her family. Life is not always fair but this type of life was not worth living. She reasoned with her son and husband to bring back Sonakshi after begging pardon from Neelam and her family but she was ridiculed for her weak approach. She was now to take decision what she wanted to do with herself and Sonakshi who she had come to know was pregnant. Even news of pregnancy had no effect on Krishna and Bhushan.

Sarita found herself at the door of Neelam with hands folded, head down with shame and tears in eyes. Hug between friends melted all evil feelings and complaints. All hurts fled in tears of two friends joined by Sonakshi who held both her mothers tightly. Sarita moved to her father's house which was locked for years since death of her parents. Sonakshi moved there in few days and in five months they had Aryan with them, their bundle of joy. Both Sarita and Sonakshi are working and looking after business left but father of Sarita which has been reestablished by them. Krishna came once to meet her but Sarita refused to meet him unless he is pardoned by Sonakshi. She sleeps well with Aryan in between her and Sonakshi. She got much more than what she left.

❐

12
Keshav

From childhood he lived a very tough and hard life. He was an orphan who served as domestic help to make his two ends meet. Getting educated was his dream but life never gave him opportunity of such a luxury. From domestic help, he travelled to an assistant in a shop of his master but salary was too meagre.

On coming of age, he got married to Sita who herself was working as domestic help but she was a refined lady whose ideas and ideals about life were very clear. She was also illiterate but educated by school called life. They worked together to make things happen and life became comfortable, though tiring. Then they were blessed with a son Gaurav and they both had dream of giving him life which they never got.

He had collected some money by the time from savings and decided to take a shop on rent but was still short of money. His master also helped but that was just too less for establishing the shop. Despite his opposition, Sita made him to sell her gold ornaments which she had brought in marriage and also what he had given. So the shop was purchased and he started in a small way, though independently. Sita left her job to take care of Gaurav to give him best what they could.

Life smiled on them and their happiest day came when Gaurav was admitted to school. He was so happy to see his name in school register as father of a student. By this time, he had learnt to sign his name in English, though he had no idea of words. Time flew and brought more good news as Gaurav was good in studies and was always in top three rankings in his class. He got distinction in Matriculation exams and then qualified for engineering course. Arranging fee was little difficult but he managed. Now son of two illiterate servants is going to have high position in society. Gaurav was also a dutiful son who understood the sacrifices made by his parents.

Their eyes were living dreams of future of Gaurav settling and bringing respect and reputation to them. That was his favourite past time and his only intoxicant as he never smoked or used any intoxicant in life. Two pairs of eyes were looking a dream but one got shut prematurely because of cancer when Gaurav was in final year. Both he and Gaurav were shattered but they supported each other out of catastrophe.

Life again started moving. Gaurav after completing education got a govt. job. High moral standard taught by Sita never left Gaurav who served as honest officer in department which was infamous of corruption. His honesty gave him reward as he was always posted in far-flung areas so as not to create impediment in smooth working system of department. Gaurav brought his first salary with him and gave it to children's home in Ambphalla and then took promise of never being given salary unless needed by him which never came. His necessities in life were too less and shop was giving him enough to take care. He had taken loan on shop from bank for education of Gaurav but never told him. He wanted to pay loan himself and not from salary of Gaurav. Educating son was his responsibility and his selfrespect would never allow him to take money from his son for that.

When Gaurav brought Alia home as the girl whom he wanted to marry, he welcomed her with open heart and she was taken in family as daughter who was always missing.

Birth of granddaughter brought unmatched happiness in his life. He saw spirit of his Sita reborn. The little angel was named Sita, though it was old fashioned by modern standard but his desire was honoured with respect by Gaurav and Alia. He started closing his shop two hours in advance to be with Sita for more times. Sita also recognised him more than even Alia who was busy with her job too.

When Sita was less than two years old she was detected with malignancy which was at inception stage and could have been cured. Money involved however was astronomical at 12 lakhs. With advance withdrawal from his GP fund and savings Gaurav could arrange only five Lakhs. Getting rest of money was difficult.

May be Gaurav could ask his father to sell shop but he knew sentimental attachment of his father with shop which was last memory of his mother. He was thinking if could have sold shop to save his Sita but that was not possible as shop was mortgaged. Time had come to reveal this to Gaurav as there was no other way out. But he was looking for one with all honesty.

It came through his regular customer Dr. Gupta who informed him that one of his patients and a very rich person is suffering from renal failure of both kidneys and can survive only if kidney transplant takes place which was depending upon someone donating his kidney. Blood group was same B positive. Hospital in Delhi was charging 30 lakhs for transplant out of which half will be given to donar.

That night was longest night in his life. Night of decision. How far he can go to save Sita. Next day he showed his desire to Gaurav to go for Tirth Yatra to Char Dham for recovery of Sita and told him he will be back after two months but told him to collect seven lakhs from Doctor Gupta with whom he had kept money, after a week. Gaurav cried as did Alia and he also. Sita started sobbing when she found everyone crying.

He returned after two months. Surgery and treatment of Sita was going on and she was recovering. He was still left with eight lakhs and one kidney. He paid four lakhs to release his shop from mortgage of bank. Rest four lakhs he deposited in fixed deposit for marriage of Sita when time would come. Gaurav never knew what his father has done for him during his life time. It was only on Uthala of his father in July 2005 that he was told about what his father has done without even saying a word and without letting them know, by Doctor Gupta who had promised to his father not to reveal the truth but it had become difficult for him to shield the truth. He gradually purchased house and named it Keshav Niwas. Spirit of his father Keshav lives their with his family particularly Sita who is now healthy and studying in Presentation Convent School.

❐

13
Airgun

Childhood was filled with playing tricks and pranks, though most of times with innocence and without desire or intention to hurt anyone. They were both friends with lot of similarities, both were good at hearts but bad in studies. Their time together was always filled with meaningless gossiping. In college also they were inseparable. No concern or worry about future when their colleagues were busy making moves for careers. Raj and Sunny knew life this way.

It was extreme winters and exams were about two months away. They were preparing for exams together. Nights were also together in house of either of them for studying. Families of both friends were happy that at least they were studying. But their time was spent less for studies and more for other things.

On a chilly night around 11 pm or so they decided that enough study had been done, full one hour, so it was time to take walk so as to remain awake. Airgun of Sunny was taken along. In early 80s security scenerio was comfortable. They went to Circular road and started firing with airgun on targets like tree or Gate of Muncipal Library. There was bulb at distance at the outpost of residence of high govt. official may be Chief Secretary. Between two friends it was better fixed who can hit that bulb by airgun shot. Both knew that was not possible from such distance. First shot aimed by Raj and it was bang on target.

With bulb hit by airgun the lone guard on the post who must be sleeping woke up and came out as also chowkidar and seeing two boys on road they understood who had broken bulb and ran towards them. Chowkidar ran towards other side to block the only way they could had run leaving then no options to jump small hill and run into graveyard towards river. Seeing them running towards graveyard the chasers stopped and pelted stones on then and then went back abusing. Both friends were in middest of graveyard in chilly night with blankets on them and a airgun which had created all problems. They had to move towards river and then take round of three kilometres to take alternative route towards Shahidhi Chowk.

Fear had gripped them moving in graveyard and it was already midnight. They heard faint voice of female from shed in graveyard which had effect of chilling their spines. Moving ahead trembling they saw to their horror a young girl tied with cloth in shed and a young boy who must have abducted her. She was pleading for mercy. It was dark except dim light coming from a pillar in shed. Mustering courage Sunny shouted at the stranger to run away lest he will be killed and Raj held airgun out towards boy. In dark it was difficult for boy to distinguish between airgun and real gun and he ran away after threatening that he is brother of dreaded criminal. It took few seconds to Sunny to realise the identity of person and the problem they have created for themselves but saving girl was more important.

The boy having left they took girl along and moved out of graveyard without talking a word to girl who was too terrified to speak. She was also resident of same locality and had been kidnapped same evening while returning home late. Both friends also had fear that if someone saw them together it would create more problems. Somehow they left the girl outside her home and reached house of Sunny. It was already 2 am. Scaling wall and entering their room was such a relief. Night which would leave imprints on their future life had passed but they were not sure about its fallout.

Two days thereafter the father of girl came to them, an aged Kashmiri Pundit. He wept inconsolably and left like that with folded hands. They did ask whether he wanted action to be taken by police and offered to stand as witness but he refused for fear of disrespect and dishonour it would bring to his daughter. After a week both friends went to area where shop of abductor was to fight with their contradiction whether he had recognised them. They took mutton from his shop. However, he hadn't identified them. Mutton they fed to street dogs on way back.

Life took full circle. After 30 years the girl came to office of Sunny with her daughter to discuss her problem. They recognised each other but only eyes spoke.

❐

14
Inspector

She was coming from her higher secondary school in Panjtirthi in her uniform. Reaching Lane towards her house in Jain Bazaar, she saw Kumar who had been following her for last about a month and passing obscene remarks. He was infamous gangster of the area who had come out on bail in murder case only few months back. She had wondered about the legal system which can let free such beasts who have no remorse. Anyway she tried to avoid him by entering a side lane. When she moved only few steps he moved fast and in to times he was by her side and had caught hold of her arm. She pleaded with him as her father had died only few months back and she was only daughter of widowed mother. But he was dead drunk and listened not.

To her utter horror, she realised that in order to avoid him she has entered side lane which is deserted and nobody was coming. She tried to pull herself away but that infuriated Kumar who slapped her. She fell down on ground with blood oozing from lips. Side of her shirt from shoulder also got torn. She tried to cover herself and cried loud for help. Two three windows opened from houses but on seeing Kumar they got shut with more speed than with what they opened. She was all alone with demon.

After about ten minutes, she reached her home with clothes torn at number of places and narrated the whole happenings to her mother. For two nights only sound in their house of mother and daughter sobbing and crying. Some ladies from neighbourhood did come but both of them were speechless and waited for ladies to depart.

It was third day when mother mustered courage to stand in morning and cooked food which she forced her daughter to take. She cried loud for first time after nightmare and wanted to jump from roof but was stopped by mother who threatened to follow her. That afternoon they resolved to fight back. But there was nobody to help two poor souls.

After two days of discussion on tears, they decided to go to a respectable person of locality who was widely respected for his courage and social works. But even he was afraid to intervene directly. It was then she was told by Monit ji that Kumar was facing four murder cases and number of other cases and was part of larger gang controlling crime underworld of city. However, he sent them to Inspector Madan who was SHO of police station, though not of their area but was having reputation of not listening to any recommendations and being dare devil. She found father in Madan who was so emotionally charged listening to her mishappening but was not in position to help as crime was outside his jurisdiction and SHO of her area was known for his corruption. He promised to do something and asked to wait.

She waited for a month and when no message came from Inspector Madan she understood that even he was afraid of Kumar and his gang. She started going to school after a month. It was very difficult time facing people but there was no choice. Now even members of gang of Kumar had started passing remarks. That was price of being an orphan she had to pay. There was none to ask help for. There was not even God.

After about three months on a chilly winter early morning there was knock on the door. She opened door with her mother looking from her back. A police constable had come with written message from Inspector Madan asking her to come to police station but asked her to come alone. She went with constable in police jeep which was parked in Bazaar. Reaching police station she saw only Inspector Madan and one more constable. She was asked to sit on chair and then Inspector Madan asked constable who had brought her to bring out from lockup "Shikar." And she saw to her horror Kumar being brought out from lockup. He was badly beaten which brought smile to her face which she has forgotten since more than three months. He was in handcuffs. Madan asked constable whose name she still remember as Satinder Singh to give her "Trapad." She couldn't understand but was handed over a leather broad belt. Madan asked her to beat Kumar to her heart's fill. She was so scared. When Madan coaxed her again and again then finally the dam of emotion breached and she beat Kumar madly. She didn't know from where she got courage and from where madness came.

After she fell down tired and saw Kumar he was bleeding from mouth because of belt injuries. The same way as she bled on that day in side lane. Inspector Madan gave her water and after sometime he said they have to take Kumar for walk. She couldn't understand but Kumar did. He started sorting and crying and begged Madan for his life. Madan asked her whether she wanted to join. She was so tired and also so happy that she wanted to fly to her mother to tell her the whole episode. She was feeling so light. She asked permission from Madan to go home who asked constable Satinder to drop her to Matador stand.

Reaching home she just fell in lap of her mother and was laughing madly. It must have taken ages for her that day to regain composer to tell her mother her outbrust and how she enjoyed the time even if it means dying next day in the hands of Kumar or his gang. That whole day passed in house totally cut from world. Night again brought fear back about backlash but then both of them slept in each others arms like it was last night of their lives.

Next day she didn't feel like going to school but her mother told her to go to her school as she had missed school last day too. When she reached Chowk Chabutra, she saw group of people gossiping with newspaper in hands. All shops were closed and shopkeepers were standing out on road. When she reached school her teacher have her copy of newspaper. First headline read "INFAMOUS GANGSTER KUMAR KILLED IN POLICE ENCOUNTER." She understood meaning of word 'Walk' of Inspector Madan. She went running back to home to inform her mother of end of their miseries.

After six years she got married. Her kanyadaan was done by Inspector Madan. Today she was again looking to obituary page of newspaper. Toady was twenty-fifth death anniversary of Kumar. She just hated his picture and wanted to beat even his picture with Trapad. Tear came in her eyes remembering her Angel who left this world four years back. Inspector Madan.

❐

15
Hijacker

Sitting in aeroplane for first time, Aryan was looking out of window. Plane taking off and the buildings becoming tiny and tinier was wonderful experience. Very soon the plane was in the clouds. He felt as if wings had grown to him. With open eyes his life flash backed to him like dream. He belonged to humble background and for everything in life he had to work hard. Nothing came on platter to him. He was only son of his parents, father working as peon in college and mother a housewife.

He faced failures mostly in life, whatever may be justification he could through for that. He was a mediocre student who was just average in studies and extracurricular activities. He, took to Boxing but never went beyond representing state. In all, there was nothing happening noteworth in his life but for desire to excel. But he never knew the way. He was into debates in college and then in university and was going for debate to Delhi, representing his state and got opportunity to travel by air as his team mate was Sanjogita, who belonged to a very rich and influential family and she didn't like idea of travelling by train on University expenses and purchased tickets for her and Aryan by air. They were accompanied by a very graceful lady, Jordia, who was the Governess of Sanjogita. As flight was not full so he got opportunity to get window seat. He felt acute sense of jealousy for Sanjogita who had all privileges and amenities in life only because of her birth in an influential and rich family and could be in skies whenever she wants.

While having food, which was served in flight, he saw some unusual activities in opposite row where a couple was sitting. Suddenly, the female shifted back and a male came in that row. Both males looked suspicious to Aryan in the way they were talking to each other by whispering and he was attracted towards socks of the male who had just shifted. His left sock was lifted as if there was something hidden therein. Out of gut feeling Aryan moved from window seat to side seat. Now, he was sitting by the side of the two. He had already unbuckled belt.

He was perplexed as what was to be done as he wasn't sure himself, so kept waiting while keeping an eye on two. Suddenly, the two got up. The person on side pulled a pistol from his socks and other was having a small knife. The person with knife shouted at everyone to put their hands behind head and lye down while person with him stood in the passage with pistol in hand. The one with knife moved towards cockpit but before he could reach there, both air hostess in front rushed in cockpit and locked it from inside. Hijacker with knife banged at the cockpit door but pilot didn't open. Hijacker with pistol shouted, "Hamid, they will open after two persons are killed. let's start that. These Bastard understand that only."

Aryan was sitting just near to place where hijacker with pistol was and one with knife was about 9 rows ahead of them. He knew that the situation is too dangerous and also knew they may have more companions, atleast the lady who had shifted back. But it was time to do what had alluded him whole life, one opportunity to become extraordinary from ordinary. He knew very well that he was putting his life to serious risk. But, heroism is born in difficult circumstances only. The only thought which came in his mind was that death is staring at him even otherwise. It was one chance of staring back in the face of death and say "I refuse to be intimidated."

All passengers were terrified at the situation and some of them have started crying. Most were praying but none was willing to fight. Suddenly, Aryan flung up and threw himself on Hijacker with pistol. He thought, that will make pistol to go out of hand of hijacker and may go to passenger or under the seats. But grip of hijacker on pistol was strong. He fell on seat but stood up soon. By that time Aryan was on him.

However hijacker got opportunity and fired which hit Aryan on his shoulder. He suddenly felt excruciating pain. But it was too late to stop now. With all his might he punched on the face of Hijacker and snatched pistol from his hand. In the meantime, hijacker with knife rushed towards him abusing. Out of confusion or fear, Aryan pointed pistol towards him and fired. He remembered, sound of shot, blood coming from the chest of rushing hijacker and then he felt on passage. In the meanwhile, second hijacker, who was hit by punch, tried to grape with Aryan. But Aryan threw him down and pointed pistol towards him. In the meanwhile, many passengers stood up and two air hostess who were at the back also came there. But, managing the hijacker was becoming difficult as, he was full of rage with anticipated death of his companion. Aryan then fired at his knee. The bullet broke the knee of hijacker and he thereafter became immobile.

The flight landed in Delhi and before the doors of plane were opened, the plane was encircled by Army vehicles and commandos. When commandos came in, one dead and one injured hijacker was removed. On information of Aryan, the lady, who was travelling with Hamid and who shifted back was identified and taken in custody. Announcement was made for everyone to remain seated. After about an hour, the Captain came out of cockpit and came to Aryan to hug him and say thanks. For all passengers, Aryan was saviour. Aryan was first to come out of plane in full glare of waiting media with camera flashing all around. Aviation Minister had himself come to the stairs of plane with garland in hand. A hero's welcome to Aryan, the new face of Civillian Heroics. He subsequently learnt that hijack drama was televised not only in India but to whole world and Captain was giving details of each moment which was being televised.

Following months saw emergence of a national hero. He was on countless TV shows. His heroics written over in countless writeups. His name and exemplary deed got mentioned by Prime Minister himself in Parliament. And finally, he got Kirti Chakra. He was offered to appear in endorsements and advertisements for huge financial consideration but, be firmly refused though, he didn't have good financial condition. He didn't want to sell his bravery and faith of whole nation on him. His award however was good enough for him to get decent job as Placement Manager in one of the top multinational companies. He finally got the opportunity to serve his parents.

❑

16
Relation Unknown

Pritam Singh had four brothers but he can exchange all of them for his friend Ali, his soulmate. They were one soul divided in two bodies. As kids they used to race with each other for reaching Gurudwara and Masjid in their village and returning back to playground after their Ardas and Namaz. Life was pure bliss. No worries. Their coming of age and marriages changed nothing. They shared their kids. Pritam loved Nazia more than his son Aulakh and same was reciprocated by Ali. It was start of rainy season when they heard that India is getting partitioned and that Hindus and Muslims have to live separate in two different countries. They laughed and shrugged their soldiers at the foolish thoughts. How can they separate, how can their families separate? Won't they fell dead without each other? What would be life without? It might be happening somewhere else but can't happen in Kotli Mian Fateh, where their ancestors lived and died, where the earth still smells of their youth. Then news started pouring in. Of frenzy on both sides. Of killings and rapes and abduction and robberies and loots and burnings. Ali shifted to Haveli of Pritam to jointly face problems which may come. They were one big family. Happy family. Nothing happened for three months and in the meantime India was divided in two countries over blood and gory. They thought they are past bad as their Maharaja had saved state from trouble, though reports of violence from few places did continue coming. Then it struck the village. People whom nobody had seen earlier starting coming. Strange clothes, strange dictum and stranger ways. Full of hatred and eager to incite and kill. They were dreaded tribals from afar place who came armed to take over Kotli Mian Fateh and the whole state to make it part of Pakistan. Each night they used to fire guns in air to scare away Hindu and Sikh population to run away. And most did run. But how could Pritam leave. Not without Ali and his family particularly his Gudia Nazia. He stayed back but allowed his brothers and their families to move to Nowshera town. He sent his wife too with promise to call her back when things settle down. Aulakh didn't go as he can't leave lap of his Chacha and Ali was in all tears begging for not removing Aulakh from him.

It was probably first week of September and little chill had started that killings of people of one religion started in village who didn't leave as they had nowhere to go. What followed was horrific as hell. There were dead bodies on the roads. Cries of women being forcibly abducted and raped. Many girls jumped in well to save honour and some were killed by their own mothers by poisoning before killing themselves. Life taken by one who gave. People were searched and pulled out of their houses and hideouts to meet death for defiance. For not running away. Pritam was afraid more for Aulakh then himself. They had one big room where Baithak used to be held. Meeting room. Ali put beddings on floor and hide Pritam in that with ladies of the house around so that nobody could find. It continued for two days but a servant informed tribal leader Hamid who pulled Pritam from behind ladies and after abusing him stabbed him in abdomen and threw him on the beds on floor telling him to die amongst ladies. Ali made all efforts and even threw himself on Pritam but was kicked aside. After Hamid and his companions left, Ali and his wife applied mud and water on the wound to stop bleeding and whole night they were crying and weeping. Pritam survived and saw Aulakh with relief whose hairs had been cut by Ali. Ali was standing with hairs of Aulakh in his hands and with folded hands and unspoken apology on lips. Pritam understood. Next night again Hamid came and finding Pritam alive was filled with rage and anger and again stabbed and wished death to infidel. Again Ali and his wife put their earthly ointment to the wound. It seemed that mother earth didn't want Pritam to die.

Third day Pritam Singh was lying on bed with wounds on both sides of abdomen waiting for his death as Hamid and his associates were not going to leave him third time. Ali came in evening and shifted him to room on first floor with wooden bed and also brought a rotting dead body from Street and burnt it to ashes in the varandah. When dawn fell Pritam could hear voice of Hamid arguing with Ali who was telling him that Sardar has died and had been cremated but Hamid was not accepting and was asking his companions to search for Sardar. His death was near. Nothing could have saved him. He saw from sides of his closed eyes someone opening door. He closed his eyes preparing for death. Time passed like eternity. Nothing happened. He could feel someone lying near him but neither he could open eyes nor touch to find. He was waiting sword to strike his neck. Door was flung open and someone shouted who is this girl lying without clothes. Rehana wife of Ali said her daughter Nazia and her husband were staying in room and asked Nazia to pull up Razai. He felt Razai being pulled up and then sounds of feet moving away. He felt relieved but very next moment he realised what had happened. Nazia was lying with him without clothes to save him. His daughter.

He was trembling with thought of humiliation and insult. He can't give this price for living. He can't take from Ali this sacrifice for friendship. His back was towards Nazia and tears were flooding the bed when Nazia put her hand on his shoulder and said Papa ji. He died of shame. Hamid and his companions left village after ensuring religious cleansing for another village to spread terror. After a week Pritam was in position to move, though with wounds badly effected and filled with puss and infection and was now leaving his village and his friend. That was fate and destiny. Ali arranged a pony for them. He bid goodbye to all but couldn't see eye to eye with Nazia. They settled finally where destiny wanted them. There was a line of border, though there was no border between them. Ali had rented fields of Pritam. He never forgot to send money to Pritam of produce of fields and Nazia never forgot to send Rakhi to Aulakh. What Partition and which Partition. Of Land not Faith.

❐

17
Preacher

He came from the fairyland. Land of thousand tales. He was ordained to cult of Sufism since his childhood and had served his master well in the path of Almighty. All different cults were working under a common council which decided to spread religion in areas where people were living with non-monotheistic religious thoughts. He found it absurd the very idea of anybody equal to Almighty or many gods. On his cult the duty was cast to spread real religion based on monotheism to land which was known in his country as Heavens on earth. He had made name for himself in religious thoughts and also in alchemy which was his second love.

Bab Sahib, his master selected him for honour to travel to Land of Heavens for spreading word of God and asked him what he needed to be taken along. He took one day and then informed Bab Sahib that he will prefer to go alone with only two bottles of his potions. When containing deadly poison and other it's antidote.

It took him six months to reach Land of Heavens on his mule named Bulbul. When he entered valley, he saw people happy and prosperity all around. There was little chance of his success. King was devoted person who had one son and one daughter and also his younger brother of age of his son whom he loved very much. He started spreading message of love of God which was taken well and in less time he was taken as Rishi. But he was careful not to propagate monotheism. Getting access to royal court was comparatively easy. King also found him learned person and worldly wise.

He tried to take king in his stride by narrating to him concepts of monotheism and the righteousness in belief in one God but King was given to religion of his forefathers and his people and didn't agree. He displayed his powers to foretell future and king impressed called his brother and children to know about their future. This was time he was waiting for. Very small needle was dosed with poison. One was concentrate which could take effect in one day, second was diluted to have effect in two days and third was more diluted to take effect in four days. Antidote was with him only. No other solution or medicine would have worked. It took him little efforts to put painless prick with needle on the hands of three youngsters. Then he produced that son will die in one day while daughter will die in two days and lastly brother will die in four days. King was shocked and angered as there was no reason for him to believe such nonsense. Rishi was put to jail immediately. He smiled and waited for his plan to work as it couldn't fail.

Sure enough son of King died first in exactly one day after prediction. King was devastated but refused to believe Rishi still. It could have been mere coincidence. But in hearts of hearts he had fear for second day prediction and called his Kulguru to have special Yagna for peace and health of his daughter. Yagna failed as it was to. Daughter of king died on the time predicted for cause unknown. King was suddenly shaken to realize the crime he had committed in arresting Rishi and not listening to him. He even didn't ask Rishi if there was a way out, in his fit for rage. His faith in Kulguru, his Yagna and even his god had shaken.

Rishi was called from prison and provided seat equal to throne of king, much higher than Prime Minister and even Kulguru. King begged him pardon and asked him forgiveness which Rishi happily did. On being asked solution to the problem, he played his cards cautiously by telling king that God is annoyed with him of making many idols parallel to him and that he wanted king to adopt to new religion which had come from Desert. King was perplexed and so was whole Darbar. King was in no position to loose his brother too, final future of kingdom after him. He offered Rishi that if his brother is saved he will adopt to new religion and so will his people.

Mission was accomplished. Death of two innocents was burden to his conscious but that was for larger benefit and in any case it was better than fighting war for religious spread. And in the way he was becoming the most important person in the kingdom. His name finally enshrined in history is ensured. There will be shrine in his name and he will be responsible for changing course of human history in the region and serving his master and his religion. Bab Sahib would be proud of him as he was on himself. His place is secured in Jannat.

With king adopting to new religion along with his family and important persons of kingdom, it was easy to spread. Free langar services were started for persons adopting to new religions. Jobs and land grants were secured for them. With royal patronage the sailing was smooth for new religion and for him getting place in history.

❐

18

Daughter of Water

She was stone. No movement except movements of thoughts. Thoughts of past. Of her divine birth, of forced marriage, of deceit in love, of curse without reason. Waiting for her salvation which is very near. She could hear the sounds of footsteps of salvation. Coming from Ayodhya. Lord was coming.

She was reminded of her divine birth. She was not born out of love but to show down the most beautiful female. She was told by Sapatrishis that Lord Brahma created her out of water and by adding all beautiful material to show down ultimate beauty. Apsara Rambha who was very proud of her beauty and habitually was insulting and embarrassing gods, angels and saints all. She was born device beauty more beautiful and attractive than Rambha. Rambha was subdued by Lord Brahma.

She grew up to be the most beautiful young girl coming of age. Mere look at her and King of gods Indra was smitten by love bug. He was in love with her. Love at first sight. He wanted nothing other than her. She accepted the proposal of him and their courtship started. Two lovers lost in each other oblivious of rest of the world. But destiny has its own ways. Her creator, her father Lord Brahma decided to marry her and looked for best match but was not satisfied. He left it to God and destiny. She was to marry one who could take the roundabout of all three worlds earlier. She was happy and consented. Nobody could beat King of gods. She would be married to her lover. All dreams coming true.

Who could had coming between her and her destiny. None. On appointed day, Indra did win. He was first to circumvent all three worlds. All gods lost as also human warriors. She was finally going to get married to Indra. All heavens. Entered Saint Narad, her brother with his weird reasonings. She always despised her brother who always was mischief monger. Trying to prove his superiority by logic by befooling all and engineering fightings and battles. She was afraid. Fears have uncanny property of taking shape if person get obsessed with them. Saint Narad was his own best. He declared that Sage Gautam was in fact the winner. She laughed. For first time Narad would be ridiculed. How dare he even thought of her getting married to that old and horrible looking Gautam whom no girl could even imagine as husband. His logic stunned all. During the time of competition, Sage Gautam had taken three rounds around cow. As cow was described as manifestation all three worlds so in fact Sage Gautam had taken round of all three worlds much earlier than Indra. All agreed. She looked helplessly to her father with hope in eyes that he would save her. He was also like others. Convinced with Narad. She was given in marriage to old sage. Her dreams shattered. She entered her home of hermit on the banks of river Mandakini. To her great relief her husband was not bit interested in physical attributes of marriage. She was saved by God from humiliation of surrendering herself before the person who could only get her hatred for being reason of her separation from Indra.

She adopted herself to new life. Resiling to her destiny.

Gautam used to get up early morning for his prayers and bathing in Mandakini and used to finish routine things before he used to come. This routine was unwritten settlement between them. One day Gautam left as per routine but came back in no time. To her most dreadful fear he demanded his right of matrimonity. Her body. She had to agree. He possessed her without even looking to tears in her eyes and her cries which didn't get voice. She turned in stone. Lifeless. Emotionless. When she regained her composure. She could smell a strange and known fragrance, the celestial one, she always found when she used to be with Indra. She saw through her divine eyes. Gautam was nowhere and standing before her was Indra. Her Indra. She was shocked. She never thought she could be cheated by Indra. The person she loved and respected. She cursed him of never living in peace.

She was remorseful and felt cheated and humiliated. When Gautam arrived she told him everything, all minute details. She opened her heart out of being cheated. Gautam was ragging in anger. He poured water in his hands from water carrier and cursed Indra of becoming crow. He again took water and cursed her of becoming of stone. She cried foul. She was being humiliated twice. By one whom she loved and by other with whom she married. Gautam realised she was not on fault but it was too late. Curse could not be undone. He modified by using power of his penance. She would remain stone till Lord Vishnu would take incarnation as Lord Ram and by touch of his feet she would be free from curse.

She had waited for centuries. Waited in stone. Gautam used to visit her everyday. More out of remorse than love for her. Now time had come. Gautam had informed Lord Ram was arriving to free her from curse so that she could again live with Gautam, the inflictor of curse on her body and soul. She had become stone inside and out both and had no desire to become Humane again. She got no one's love. She was always alone. True to her name. Never ploughed. Ahilya. Never ploughed by love. Subject of ridicule without fault. Daughter of Water. One of Panchkanaya. Devi Ahilya.

❐

19
Manthra

She was limping her way in the palace corridors trying to reach her Shri Queen early to announce the coming of her son Jewel of her eye, future King of Ayodhya. Today was happiest day of her life. Her dreams fullfilled. The purpose of her achieved. She was assured of place in ultimate heaven Vaikuntha. That's what she learned back in her country and dedicated her life to serve Shri Queen as Parvasi Chaya.

When she entered the royal palace as maid in the service of then Queen it was honour bestowed on her lowely placed tribe. She was hardworking and dedicated and her rise in palace power structure was phenomenal. She had been bestowed by God the power to convince even adversaries with her unlawful reasoning. She aspired to be sent for rigorous trying to becoming Parvasi Chaya to Queen or Princess. She didn't get married for that reason.

While she was still young, destiny gave her opportunity to prove herself and prove she did. Queen Ajanlaya accidently put her feet on sleeping saint on bank of great river Sindhu while going for early morning bath. Fault was not her. Sadhu Pinala was sleeping on the banks of river and it was still dark. But Sadhu Pinala was full of anger and rage that Queen couldn't see down to find a human sleeping on way. Curse was inevitable and it came. Queen was to became hunchback so that see can't see upward. All hell broke loose. She pleaded with Pinala and tried to convince him of taking curse back as Queen was not at fault. Pinala saw the reasoning and logic but he couldn't have undone curse. He offered to redirect the curse if anyone was willing to take it instead of Queen. She volunteered. Queen was saved but she became hunchback Kubarhi.

Queen Ajanlaya was changed woman after the incident. She was full of gratitude for her and her sacrifice. She asked her to demand anything. She asked for eternity through service of Queen as per traditions of Kakeiyi. Becoming Parvasi Chaya. Wish was granted. Queen promised her that in case Queen gave birth to daughter she will be her Parvasi Chaya. That was biggest honour. Being Parvasi Chaya means to remain with Princess, her Shri, for whole of her life as shadow dedicating herself to nothing but welfare of Shri and if she performed well she was assured of heavens Vaikuntha. She was sent for training to be Parvasi Chaya. And was taken by Queen as her sister. She was special. Her two brothers were taken in royal army as soldiers. Another great honour bestowed upon the family.

She returned after four years to the palace from training. Queen had given birth to a beautiful princess Kakeiyi, her Shri. Queen put the little princess in her lap. She was Parvasi Chaya of little princess with whom she had to remain like shadow for whole of her life. Nothing else mattered other than welfare of her Shri.

It was her decision to get her Shri trained as warrior much to disliking of all including king but queen had her way. Her decision for Kakeiyi prevailed who became ultimate warrior. Invincible in battle. She led army of Kakeiyi in eight battles and won all as also appreciations from her enemies and gods. She was a feared warrior. She had battle scars on her face adding to her beauty. Kings and Princes of whole Aryavarth wanted to marry her but she chose king of Ayodhya Dhashrath, already married. He was renowned for his warrior skills and was suitable match.

Marriage was quite a lavish affair and post marriage she also shifted to Ayodhya as Parvasi Chaya of her Shri now the second Queen of Ayodhya. Entering palace however was not pleasant thing for her and her Shri. Though king was dedicated and fond of Kakeiyi but the elderly Queen Koushalya had not taken kindly of new intruder in royal palace whom king was giving more attention to the extent of ignoring elder queen. What started was palace intrigues to the extent of attempts to kill her. She saved her Shri by her intelligence. Kakeiyi was sent to battles with the hope she would die but she came victorious. Koushalya got king married to a young and very beautify princess of small state Sumitra with the hope that attention of king towards Kakeiyi will get distracted but she failed here too.

When all three queens gave birth to children she got assured of her Shri becoming Raj Mata and scoring over ever scheming Koushalya despite her Bharat younger to Koushalya's son Ram by four days. That was for two reasons. King Dhashrath having given promise to Kakeiyi's father that son of Kakeiyi would be king whether he would be eldest or not. Second was the two promises Dhashrath had given to Kakeiyi on battlefield when she saved his life from Asura confederate by risking her life and she had huge gash across her face while taking full force of Lance thrown out on Dhashrath.

She despised Ram who was trained and educated by his mother to always give feeling of being good. Honey-coated. Once he hit here with iron stick with such force that her knee was broken and she never recovered from that. She was limping because of injury given by Ram because she was giving mango to son of her Shri and refused when Ram demanded that. Even her Shri didn't support her and overlooked the issue as mistake by child but how could she forget the contempt and hatred in eyes of Maryada Purshotam Ram, doer of Justice or so did Brahmins claimed under influence of Koushalya. She had only hatred for Ram as much as she had devotion for her Shri and her son. She waited for Bharat to become king for justice to be done to her for all injustices met by her. She was however very apprehensive about Koushalya and her brother who had come to stay with her for six months now. Koushalya got opportunity when Bharat asked for permission of king to visit his maternal grandfather with whom he was attached. Koushalya had to remove Shatrugana the younger son of Sumitra who was devotee of Bharat and won't allow anything to happen against interest of Bharat and who always acknowledged and treated Bharat as future king in view of commitment of King Dhashrath to father of Queen Kakeiyi.

Koushalya convinced King Dhashrath to send Shatrugana along with Bharat to give him company. This was apparently innocent and was readily accepted. Besides all Princes were married now and Bharat and Shatrugana would find time to live with their brides. They left along with their wives and entourage.

That was opportunity Koushalya was looking for. She had all learned men of Durbar on her side who convinced king that as per traditions of his clan the famous Raghuvansh the eldest son can only be king and that Queen Kakeiyi loves Ram even more than Bharat and won't object to Ram being choosen as heir apparent. King fell prey and declared Ram to be his successor and heir apparent. He did in absence of

Bharat on advice of Koushalya that this will give pleasant surprise to Bharat.

She was stunned. Despite all her training and intelligence she had been outwitted by Koushalya with the help of court priests. Kakeiyi was undress shock. She couldn't believe that her king would do injustice to her. By Lord Rudra this was ultimate back stabbing. She was clueless what to do to force king to live up to his commitment. She went to king to remind him of his promise to her father of crowning son of Kakeiyi only as king. Dhashrath was too adamant now, also for the reason that he had already announced the decision. Kakeiyi had lost her first battle to king and to Queen Koushalya.

She cried in the lap of her Parvasi Chaya and prayed for something to be done for the sake of justice to Bharat. Parvasi Chaya had little time to plan. But she drew her strength for rigorous training and planned for second attack. Indirect one. She told her plan to her Shri Queen who agreed after initial reluctance. The dice was cast now. Kakeiyi went to Kop Bhawan. The wailing hall. King came to stop her cries and wailing. She reminded king of two promises given to her in battle. King had to give desired boons.

She took her boons, as advised by Parvasi Chaya, one that Bharat should be king and second that Ram should go to jungle for 14 years. Boons granted. Dhashrath pleaded for release of boons but Kakeiyi didn't budge as per advice of Parvasi Chaya. Ram went to jungle along with elder son of Sumitra and his wife Sita. She awaited coming of Bharat for coronation. Today he was coming along with Shatrugana. Her dreams fullfilled now she was assured heavens. King Dhashrath dies because of shock but it hardly mattered for her. Her Shri Queen will become Raj Mata.

Bharat proved to be too emotional. He failed both his mother and Parvasi Chaya by refusing to be annoinated and made efforts to get Ram back which of course failed. He came back to be caretaker king till Ram would come back. She had lost worldly battle despite winning. Her Shri Queen still didn't become Raj Mata but she was satisfied she had done great justice to her duty as Parvasi Chaya. She was abused by Shatrugana but she was above this all. She was trained to stand by her Shri Queen and she almost won crown for her and her son. She would die satisfied. She was first female villain of Bharat Manthra.

❐

20
Daughter of God

She was waiting for the love of her life. He was coming after eight years after leaving her and his people for education and warrior training from best Asura Gurus in South Confederate. She was too young at that time about 12 years of age but hopelessly in love with Jullandar, her childhood friend and companion. Those deep blue eyes which reflect the pain he had undergone all his life, still haunts her. How she will face him. May be she will drop dead at the first sight of Jullandar. But she was willing to die after having mere one look of him.

He came and she missed her heartbeat. He was not riding horse but lion. How could that happen. She knew he was brave but this was suicidal. The whole Asura community thundered with applauds. Everyone was raising slogans praising the arrival of The Leader who would save them from humiliation the great Asura community had to undergo at the hands of Sura community with support of invaders Devas. Sura and Asura as two communities have always occupied the territory of Bharat without annoying each other. To the extent they share common gods. Some fair coloured as Suras like Vishnu and some dark coloured like Asuras as Shiva. But all changed by arrival of Devas from mountain who created rift between two communities by taking sides with Suras. Many leaders of Devas had married Sura women and fathered their children.

Soon after his arrival, Jullundar was declared leader and king of Asura by the resident Kalnemmi, her father. She found her companion and love whereas Asuras found their honour and saviour. After consolidating his position in the Asura Kingdom, Jullundar proposed to her father for marriage with her which was accepted as honour by him. There was no end to her joy. Her dreams had come true. She would never ask for anything from God. But desires always have tendency to surprise. Her desires also caught her. The desire for safety and honour of her husband. Her whole world started and end with Jullandar only.

She had immense faith in Lord Vishnu. Unlike for Asura queen. Her community had always prayed before Lord Shiva for powers and boons. She was always attracted towards Lord Vishnu. May be she always related qualities attached with Lord Vishnu with her father Kalnemmi. And Lord was also very kind and reciprocating. Now was time to get boon from Lord for safety of her husband and his glory. She entered very harsh Tapasaya to please Lord Vishnu. She succeeded after one year and Lord appeared in person and asked her for boon. She asked for glory to her husband and that he should be never defeated or killed by anyone. Lord granted boon to his devotee, his daughter, his faithful. He said her husband would neither lost any battle nor can be killed so long she remained faithful to him. She agreed with smiles. She can never think of anyone else.

In due course, Jullandar expanded his kingdom defeating his enemies mainly Suras and tribes and became to hilly warriors Devas. He attacked their capital and defeated and vanished their King Indra and was proclaimed ultimate leader of Asura. Sada Shiva. Always Shiva. His incarnation.

He provided administration which was responsive and there was all-round development of Asura community. All was good. But not Suras and Devas who conspired to kill Jullandar but how could words and boon of Vishnu fail. Way had to be found by Vishnu himself as also Shiva who had to join to face the threat called Jullandar. Devas spread rumours that Jullandar wanted to kidnap consort of Shiva the eternal Shakti Parvati to provoke Shiva to battle Jullandar as it was impossible for anyone to fight with Lord Shiva. They succeeded and battle started between Shiva and Sada Shiva. And another battle started between her and her destiny. She sat before idol of her Aradaya Lord Vishnu praying. Her chastity was rock steady. There was no way Shiva could even harm her Jullandar.

Battle was even between two of the greatest warriors but the situation was fast changing. Jullandar had support of her wife with her boon and Shiva was having Parvati the Eternal Shakti on his side. She was proving better than Parvati with boon of Lord Vishnu and Jullandar had the edge. Asura was looking to coming of new god, human god. Shiva was becoming weak as also the old system of Trimurti. Whole world was trembling with use of psychological weapons. Tandav had lost to prayers of Sati and her boon.

Devas rushed to their saviour Lord Vishnu to save the world and world order. They had unwittingly initiated the downfall of Lord Shiva. What a mistake. They underestimated both Jullandar and his devoted wife. Lord Vishnu had to find way to save Lord Shiva more than saving Devas or Suras. He can't allow the world to be without Lord Shiva whose mortality will end if something didn't happen soon. But nothing could happen so long she remained faithful to her husband and she couldn't forsake her husband at any cost. Everything was messed up. He had to do something to his proclaimed daughter which no father had ever imagined. Was he willing to pay the price of his boon which had become curse for everyone including him? He had to become Shiva and drink poison to save world. Nothing else could help. Only he knew Mohini, the knowledge to take anyone's image and appear like one.

She was in temple praying when door opened and her husband entered. Wounded but alive and breaming with pride. He had defeated Shiva but didn't kill him. He was now Lord Jullandar. She fell at the feet of her father her Lord Vishnu to thank for victory. He made unusual demand of making love to celebrate victory. She politely told him to first tend to wounds but he insisted and she didn't want to spoil the occasion for the love of her life. She obliged and they made love. In the battlefield suddenly Jullandar felt as if all his energy and power had left his body. He was lifeless unable to raise his weapon. Shiva found opportunity and thrust his Trishul. Thus fell Sada Shiva with smile on his lips. Satisfaction of fighting against Lord himself and now going to Heavens. She was free now but felt little strange in the arms of her husband. He was cold and unlike himself. She again saw in his eyes. They were not blue. What was this. Who was he. She cried foul and he changed his appearance.

Her Lord Vishnu was before her. She was cheated by her Lord whom she always treated father. He defiled her. Took her chastity. She was no more faithful to Jullandar though by deceit.

She asked why. No answer. She cried and wept. Still no answer. She got the answer in silence. What had happened to Jullandar. So this was all to get rid of her boon. What boon where a father can care none and dishonour the daughter to get victory in battle. Jullandar was no more. She had no reason to live. Lord again showed his magnanimity by asking her to ask for boon. She wanted none. She cursed the Lord that he will face same humiliation and what happened to her will happen with his wife too. He said she would be treated as his wife instead of daughter by all in the shape of Tulsi plant. She laughed with contempt. He didn't want her to be even known as Sati Vrinda wife of Sada Shiva Jullandar. She took one long breath and fell down dead at the feet of The Lord. He was still stun. What had struck. Even with all his wit He had no answer.

❒

21
Mai Bhago

It was hot summer of 1705 and she had gone to the village well to get water. For a young girl of 18 years of age, she was full of dreams and valour. Unlike girls of her age, her dreams were about path of oneness with God, path of liberation, path of freedom, path of faith and honour, the path shown by great Gurus which was now being led by revolutionary Guru Govind Singh who had given new vision to young Sikh religion of Saint Soldier. You have to be true Sikh by doing both duties together. Being a saint and also a soldier at the same time. Many didn't understand but followed command. She understood and followed. Sainthood was not about deserting, it is about getting involved and still remaining aloof.

While she was drawing water, she saw about 40 soldiers badly exhausted approaching her. She could realise from their looks that they were thirsty and were exhausted. All were wearing traditional Sikh soldiers war dress. She prepared herself to the honour of offering water and Sattu she was carrying with her tied to corner of her dupatta to the soldiers of the Panth. After quenching thirst of the guests, it was now time for her to quench her thirst, the thirst to know about battle, about great Guru whom she didn't have honour to see. About the honour of company of Guru.

To her horror, she was told that men she had served water and Sattu had deserted Guru Govind Singh who was surrounded by Mughal forces four villages away with no little chance of survival and these soldiers had run away to save their lives. She blasted them and put them to shame of doing the most dishonourable act. She thundered that they had not abandoned great Guru but their salvation. Death at the altar of Panth and Guru would had brought them glory in this life and salvation hereafter. They realised what they had done and asked for forgiveness and guidance.

She now recalled the martial training given to her by her father Malo Shah who prepared her in true warrior tradition. He was lead soldier of army of Guru. She was prepared in tradition to sacrifice herself in the path of glory of Panth.

She hurriedly went home and was back in no times in her full battle attire and on her horse. Offering herself to lead the group, she infused new valour to the soldiers who stated raising war cry of Bole So Nihal Sat Shri Akal.

They reached the village and could go to entrenched Guru and his few bodyguards left. She bowed before living God. The dream had come true. She washed the feet of Guru with her tears. Persuading great Guru to leave while allowing group led by her to stop Mughal forces took time but great Guru accepted in the interest of Panth.

She along with group laid seize near a dry well of the village. Mughal forces were also exhausted of thirst and fatigue and were looking for water. When they saw the group near well. They understood that well was with water which was being guarded by Sikh soldiers. They preferred to quench their thirst before continuing pursuit of Guru. Warnings and threat of surrender to her met with expected response and battle started. Kind of battle which was not witnessed. All 40 Sikh soldiers died and 129 Mughal soldiers were also killed. She was wounded massively and was left to die by enemy. To the horror of Mughal General Sadah Khan, the well was empty. The rest of soldiers already exhausted refused to move. Absence of water and battle for last four hours had completely drained them and they pulled back. She was closing eyes with sense of pride. Her Guru was safe. She was dying with satisfaction of having transformed 40 apparent deserters to 40 most important martyrs in Sikh history.

Her Guru was very kind and his kindness and blessings saved her and now after two months after recovering from wound she was before her Great Guru. She was asked for any reward by Guru ji for her services. She chose and she chose wisely. She asked for company of Guru and she got it in abundance. She was made chief bodyguard of Guru. Always with him; drinking nectar of words of wisdom of Guru, having his blessings.

She was first female Saint Soldier follower of great Guru. She was Mai Bhago, symbol of strength and bravery, of dedication and valour.

❐

22
Queen of Heartz

Born to the royal family of Lohara which lay in the Pir Panchal range of mountains to King Simharaja who was married to Hindu Shahi dynasty of Kabul. She was crippled by birth and as such couldn't get married till she was 28 years old, considerable age in 9th century. King of Kashmir Ksemagupta was surrounded by enemies and was unable to manage kingdom which was under attack by tribal warlords.

It was the year 950 AD and she was 28 years old and getting married to King Ksemagupta in lieu of military help promised by her father to save Ksemagupta from his enemies. Ksemagupta was extremely good looking and addicted to women, gambling and jackal hunting. She was carried to royal palace on back by female servants as she could not walk.

She made good of her disability and ordinary looks by her political astuteness and brilliant strategic manoeuvring to the extent that the king became totally dependent on her and ordered himself to be addressed as Diddakshema. He even got coins minted with his name Diddakshema inscribed on them. She was not the only wife though and king had another wife Chanderlekha who was daughter of the powerful Prime Minister Phalguna. She gave birth to son Abhimanyu and on the occasion invited her maternal grandfather Bhima Shahi, ruler of Kabul instead of her father for Namkaran ceremony of the child which was political master stroke and firmly put her seat of power.

Unfortunately, for her, King Ksemagupta died in 958 AD during a jackal hunting. She was prepared by officials to commit Sati along with other queen but at the last moment she avoided self-immolation with the help of Raj Prohit saying she has to live to protect her son. Chanderlekha however committed Sati and her father fled to Poonch fearing for his death.

She made Abhimanyu as child king and herself as regent to take control of state. Faced with grave situation, she decided to act tough and third day after ascending to crown as regent ordered killing of 867 royal officials and helpers, she was having suspicion of conspiring against her. This created sense of fear in the Durbar and temporarily stopped all conspiracies. Rumors were spread in the kingdom that she got hearts out of living humans by slicing their chest and that she was witch. She made no attempt to deny such rumors as those suited her with new found tough and cruel image.

Peace was not lasting though with revolt from nephews of her husband Mahiman and Patala who tried to kill her and her son in temple. She initially agreed for truce and invited them for negotiations where she tricked them to death. Thereafter, she came on her and had thousands of people killed publically on mere suspicion. Her minister Naravahana executed the tasks on her behalf.

She sent her general Yashodhara on war, who won with neighboring Kingdom but didn't kill the enemy as ordered. On way back he was treated with contempt and disregards, despite being victor and he revolted immediately with the help of many nobles. She managed to defeat them with the help from ministers Naravahana and Rakka and not only rebels but their family members were also brutally killed to dissuade and such misadventures in future.

But the person who became close to her was always cursed or so did masses thought. She got disillusioned with Naravahana over period of time and started ignoring him which was not tolerable to great warrior who chose to commit suicide. Rakka also met same fate leaving the Queen alone.

Left with no support and enemies uniting again, she decided to recall Phalguna who came back and subdued her enemies mainly tribal Damaras. Her misfortunes however failed to leave her as her son Abhimanyu died in 972 AD leaving three minor children. Eldest Nandigupta was crowned and she continued as regent.

She now devoted her time to build memorials for her son and temples and to provide able administration but her bad luck continued to haunt her as Nandigupta also dies in 973 AD followed by his brother Tribhuvangupta who met the same fate. Rumor of Queen being cursed got further flare.

She crowned Bhimagupta her third grandson in 975 but before things could stabilize her Prime Minister Phalguna died. Some said it was engineered by her. There was still another twist left to come in her life. When she was in her fifties there entered a young man from Poonch, Tunga, who was initially employed as letter carrier by her but rose to become Prime Minister which he remained for 40 years after death of Didda. Folklore of her being lover to Tunga started doing rounds even during their lifetimes with no denial by them. She at least found solace in the company of Tunga who was 20 years younger to her. She devoted her last three decades in provide effective governance and ruled country in her own name with iron hands after Bhimagupta died in mysterious circumstances in 981.

She ruled for 22 years in her own name and died in 1003 at the age of 79. She created an affective military and administration so when Mohammad Ghazni attacked Kashmir twice in 1015 and 1023 both time he was defeated by King Samgramaraja because of strong army as also because of strong administration created by her. She was Didda, Queen of Kashmir. She was called queen of hearts by her subjects though with contempt for rumors that she used to take heart out of victims while they were still alive.

❐

23
Durga

Riding on white elephant Banraj, she was looking ahead towards the huge army which Emperor Akbar of Delhi had sent under command of Behram Khan to subdue Mandala. Estimates given to her was about 80000 soldiers. She looked to dedicated 16500 of her soldiers and her elite Laxmi Sena of female warriors of 920 ready to fight for the independence and honour of their motherland even in the face of total inhalation. They had come to defend her resolve and commitment to honour and independence knowing of little chance of going back to their families. Father had left sons and daughters, husbands their wives, sons their parents with hopes of seeing them only in next life. In true Rajput traditions, they were together on the path to glory, on the path to death.

She got married to King Dalpatishah of Gadha Mandala four years back and came to royal palace as shy bride of 16 years. She was truly in love with her husband, a true warrior and able administrator who was loved by his subjects and respected even by his enemies. It was time of Mughal expansion with support of number of Rajput kings who had accepted subjugation of Akbar but there were many few like king Dalpatishah who were holding on their own. With him around even Mughal forces with huge number and infrastructure could still not have courage to start direct conflict with Mandala.

The things changed however in 1576 with death of King Dalpatishah in sudden fever and with there being no heir the mantle fell upon her to take control of state. She was doing her best but she had limitations. The allies started deserting and the state got weakened. This was open invitation to Mughals to invade and Akbar took no longer time to oblige. Now she is facing sea of army from north threatening to inhilate her kingdom and subjects.

She could had avoided conflict by accepting conditions set out by Behram Khan requiring her to accept subjugation of Akbar, to pay subjugation tax, to maintain minimum army with permission and to allow free propagation of Islam in her territory. She called the grand council to take their advice which put the onus on her to take decision and all took the vow to stand by her decision. Decision she took. Decision to fight. Decision not to be subjected to subjugation. Decision to choose free death over chained freedom. All stood up and stood by.

She waited for two months in the fort for enemy to retreat because of frustration and fatigue as fort was impregnable but reverse happened. Food stock of her was almost finished whereas Mughals had steady food supply line. There was no option left then to fight in open and here she was. In open ready to fight and ready to die in the name of honour and freedom.

Battle continued for whole day and she proved her warrior skills by killing scores of enemy soldiers from back of her elements by accurate use of her archery skills. By dawn the situation had slipped out of her hands. She was outnumbered heavily and there was dissension in the temporary soldiers too. Her casualties were more than 8000 to around 13000 of Mughals. But Mughals could still withstand the higher number of casualties.

By evening it was clear that her army will be completely inhilated and she will be caught as war criminal. This was time to take decision. She again didn't fail herself.

Decision she tool again. Not to allow enemy the glory of having Maharani of Mandala as prisoner of war and facing humiliation of royal trial. She chose the path of sacrifice. Laying down her life at the alter of freedom. With final war cry Jai Janani she slit her throat with her sword. Thus fell from Banraj the greatest of female warrior India had seen. Her blood fell on the earth and shined like jewel. Motherland couldn't withstand the agony of having blood of Daughter of the Soil on her bosom. Darkness fell.

She was Durgavati, Queen of Gadha Mandala.

❐

24
Breast Tax

Treasure found in strong rooms of Sri Padmanabhaswamy temple in Thiruvanthapuram estimated to be worth at least five trillion rupees enough for India to get rid of all its debts multiple times, had shocked the nation and the curiosity of the masses has been generated to know about the source of such a mammoth treasure. The wealth had flown in the temple vaults since 15th century with administration of temple in the hands of closed group known as Ettara Yogam (Council of Eight and Half). It was so as it had eight and half votes with seven votes to powerful Pootti Brahmins one vote to Nair family and only half vote to royal family.

This council was put in charge of eight provinces of whole Travancore region and very soon royal family was marginalized to a greater extent and war erupted between King Marthanda Varma who after initial exile, could manage to kill eight Lords with the help of neighboring kings and proclaimed himself to be undisputed king of Travancore. By that time, the treasure of temple was already overflowing with taxes collected from masses by brutal means mostly from Dalit community.

Example was, imposing tax on Dalit women to cover their naked breasts. They were debarred from moving out in public with covered breasts unless they pay tax known as Mulakaram. This was one of about 100 taxes imposed whose collections would go to Padmanabhaswamy temple along with taxes on pepper and other spices. Furthermore, the war money also went to vaults of temple.

King Marthanda Varma in an intelligent move surrendered his kingdom to Lord Padmanabhaswamy and proclaimed himself to be servant of Lord. So, Travancore become Kingdom ruled by Lord himself through his servant. This made it impossible for other kingdoms to attack kingdom of God rather they regularly paid gold and gifts to temple which again went to vaults and Travancore became safe and rich.

History wouldn't have been same but for a courageous young Dalit woman and her emancipated and encouraging husband. Nangeli was born in Ezhava Dalit community who had to face the inhuman treatment of being subjected to Mulakaram. She was neither in position to afford tax nor was willing for such humiliating treatment to women and decided to revolt.

She refused to either cover her bosom or pay the breast tax. To encourage other women of lower caste, she would move out with covered breasts along with her husband and counsel the village folks to revolt against Mulakaram to the annoyance of ruling class who took this as defiance of royal dictate and encouraging revolt.

On being informed, the king sent Pravathiyar (Village Officer) of Travancore to ask her to pay tax. When Pravathiyar along with soldiers reached her house and demanded Mulakaram she went inside and chopped her

breasts and gave them to Pravathiyar on a banana leaf to present to king. She literally bled to death after seriously suffering from open wounds soon after. Her husband Kandappan who all along supported his wife committed Sati on her pyre becoming first husband in recorded history to ascend the pyre of a dead wife. The other overwhelming self-sacrifice by Avarna Ezhava couple gripped the land and items regime forever and the place is known today as Mulachiparambu (land of breasted woman) ever since. The kind of self-sacrifice and furious protests were the first fight for women liberation anywhere in the world.

The news reaching king and public anger and revolt eminent, the king abolished the dreaded tax very next day. Sacrifice of Nangeli and her husband gave dignity to the women of lower castes in south. Treasure of Shri Padmanabhaswamy belongs to such persons and should be used for their welfare and upliftment.

❒

25
Half and 14

Ghazal was brought to court in full police escort. Today was the day of filing of charge sheet against her for mass murder of eight persons. Court was jam packed, more with media persons who had come to cover the most gruesome murder ever committed by a female, of killing not one but eight persons in one go by firing through AK 47. She was branded as terrorist and inhuman and a living demon, etc. but when she got out of police van in simple white cotton suit, most of persons were impressed by her beauty and her majestic gate. There was authority in the way she walked and there was internal peace which was reflecting on her face. She was a confident women immensely proud of herself and what she did.

The proceedings otherwise were routine one, except for an application by Nitiya, a freelance journalist, for holding interview with Ghazal and the leading lawyer of state Rakesh was in court to argue that application. Judge was in delima taking application as how can he direct an accused to face interview against her wishes. When application was taken, judge asked Ghazal whether she will like to be interviewed. Ghazal looked straight in eyes of Nitiya but could find only sympathy for herself which was new feeling for Ghazal since the day two months back when she fired upon and killed eight persons. "I have no objections" was the only sentence she could speak. So things became easy for judge to decide in favour of Nitiya, with little persuasive arguments of Rakesh.

Nitiya met Ghazal next day in her jail cell to know from her truth and to present her side of story to public. Story of a woman who is condemned before trial. Nitiya knew the duty she has taken upon herself is onerous and not easy but then that's the way she always has been in life. Rebellious and dare devil. It took her little effort to break initial reluctance and silence of Ghazal and she finally broke when Nitiya asked about her daughter Sargam.

It was all tears and it took quite a time for Ghazal to regroup herself and start the talking. She was born in middle-class family. Her earliest memories were of a doting father taking her on his scooter every evening for ride and then getting her sweets and chocolates and whatever she demanded. Her mother always tried to reason with her father to not spend beyond his financial capacity for their only child but her father's love knew no limitations and constraints not even financial. As a child also she was very beautiful and was always centre of attraction wherever she went. On top of it she was brilliant in studies and wanted to become a scientist. Her father wanted her to take medical line but she insisted in her choice and a caring father agreed. In university, she was adjudged best fresher and was most sought after, for all boys but she never paid any heed to them. She was focussed on her aim.

It was in her second year that she met Suresh who was a class senior to her. He belonged to a rich family and was having charming personality, though he was not a brilliant student like her. But she was attracted towards him when he took initiatives. Their love was like hot stream meeting cold stream. It progressed in leaps and in no times she crossed limits which she should have never. She realised when she found herself to be pregnant. She was horrified and was shivering how she would face her father who lived his life only on her happiness. She talked to Suresh who said she shouldn't worry and he would talk to his family and they would get married. She got reassured and thought everything would be fine. She however told her mother everything who in turn told her father. She unexpectedly found support from her father who stood by her and told her that he would go and meet family of Suresh. She however told him to wait as Suresh would talk to his family first.

Days pass and then weeks but Suresh was just giving one excuse after another. In the meantime, she reached fourth month of her pregnancy and as per doctor it was now not possible for her to even terminate. On that day, she decided to meet parents of Suresh herself as he had not met her for almost a week. She alone with her father went to residence of Suresh to get her life but she got only humiliation and insult. Father of Suresh threw some money at her face and asked her to get lost. Her father was also insulted. She was told that Suresh had already left for USA and won't come back. When she came out of that hell she could only see blackness and suddenly she heard sound of something falling on ground. She turned back and realised that was her father. He was shifted to hospital but collapsed in three days and then within one month her mother also died because of brain heamorrhage. Her one wrong step had destroyed whole family and there she was with an illegitimate child in her womb whom she couldn't even destroy. She regrouped herself and have birth to her child. Sargam who was as beautiful girl as her mother. Her beauty made Ghazal worried. She just hoped Sargam had different luck at least.

Ghazal stopped to take breath. She sipped water from glass and then started again.

She joined service as junior scientist after finishing her Masters. Atleast she fulfilled this dream. Sargam grew to be more beautiful then her. Ghazal told Sargam everything about her on her 15th birthday so that Sargam never commit mistake which she had.

It was a Saturday, she vividly remembered, when she got information of Sargam been kidnapped from school by infamous gangster Narayan Bali through his gang members. Ghazal went running to house of Narayan to rescue Sargam but she was not allowed to enter. She went to police and court and politician and whom not for four days but none helped as there was no evidence. A mother was running for her child in this merciless world and in night she was only crying outside her house as she had no strength to enter house without Sargam. After four days, Sargam came home one night and her condition told Ghazal what had happened to her. Mother cursed God for what life she has been given. That night itself she left city with Sargam.

Ghazal returned to city with stone face after a month. She had put Sargam in boarding school and deposited all her money in fixed deposit in name of Sargam including money she got selling her house and interest on money was more than enough for studies and boarding charges for Sargam for future. She could forgive person who destroyed her life but in no way she could spare person who defiled her daughter. She had to kill Narayan for revenge and also to give message to persons who take women as a thing only.

She went to police chief to take his help and told him her story. He promised to help but had a indecent proposal for her, of spending one night with her. She had no desire to live now except taking revenge. She succumbed but her ill luck was still not leaving her. Police chief turned his back and she soon realised she had been used. But revenge is so strong a feeling that it knows no pain or moral. She went to any person with whom she had hope. Some refused and some did same as police chief. In all she was physical misused by 14 people, exploiting her burning desire of revenge.

And finally she got her opportunity in unexpected way. She was walking on side of street when she was hit by a speeding vehicle. She only felt big jerk and then blackout.

When she regained consciousness she was in a palatial house with two doctors attending her. When she got up she saw a middle-aged man standing with folded hands "I am really and extremely sorry for accident sister. Mistake was of my son. Please forgive him." He pulled his son who was hiding at his back. She saw a boy of hardly 14 or 15 years of age. She pulled boy towards her and hugged him and said "it's OK. He is son to me too." She wanted to go but was compelled by family to stay till she fully recovered. Man and his wife were always with her taking care of her even minor needs. She felt the joy of family in those days and was specially attached to boy Anuj who was as innocent as Sargam. She remained there for about two weeks and during this time she was treating with all respect and honour and as family member. Man used to call as sister and was very considerate and so was his wife. Anuj use to be with her during evening after his school and golf sessions and listening to stories from her. When she got well and told them that she would be leaving next day, they were all perturbed genuinely. Man requested her to stay with them as it was her home too but she knew very well her aim is not to live in peace but to take revenge. In night her foster brother came to her. "What can I do for you sister? You have done huge favour by not reporting to police on accident beside in short time you have showered so much love upon him that he is crying that you are leaving" he said. Ghazal had tears in eyes and with heavy throat said: "I also love Anuj. He is such an innocent and loving kid. I am living in this city and will come oftenly to meet my family. But I need nothing" But in last line there was so much pain that her brother immediately understood that she was in some sought of trouble. It took lot of persuasion and finally swearing in name of Anuj that Ghazal spoke out everything, every bit of it. The storm within had finally broken out and all pain came out which was suppressed all life as there was none to listen. When she stopped she saw all her pain and sufferings on face of her brother who was full of anger and distress on what had happened to her. "What do you want?" he asked. "Revenge and only revenge. I have destroyed my life for that" was the reply. He promised to help.

Next day she left. For next about a month passed and she didn't hear from her new brother. He might have forgotten and honestly Ghazal had no hope or expectations from any person. Then he came one morning with a senior police officer. He told her that he had taken orders from concerned minister to take action against Narayan and that he would be arrested and prosecuted in court and she would finally get her revenge. "How can I allow this. It would mean bringing Sargam as witness and making her identity known to all. And beside I don't want court trial or jail to that bastard. I want to kill him with my own hands" Ghazal said. Her brother went out with police officer. She could see them arguing in lawn outside. After about half hour her brother came and told her to be ready in two days.

On third day during late evening she got up to attend door bell and found two persons in a jeep. They took name of her brother and told her that they had been sent by him and asked her to sit in jeep. In jeep she was handed over AK 47 and procedure to use. It was kept loaded on automatic mode where it could fire all 30 bullets in one go only with putting finger on trigger. She got call on her mobile. Her brother was on other side. "I have called Narayan and his seven associates who kidnapped Sargam in his out house for a business deal. This AK 47 belongs to one of his PSO who was also involved and would be there. They would be having their weapons too. You have only one chance of firing moment you enter door which will be open as they are waiting for me. Remember if even one survive I will be dead too. Keep cool and don't waste time. Try to leave immediately and you would find a vehicle in next lane which will take you out of city. Never come back. Live in peace with Sargam, Good luck." Ghazal wanted to thank

God for first time having sent her brother to her life. And then all emotions and thinking went out. She was woman of steel, seething with contempt and anger. She threw her mobile in drain on way to remove trace of her brother.

When she entered door, she saw Narayan sitting on sofa and seven persons sitting on floor around him. They were all drinking. She wanted to spit on face of Narayan before killing him but had no time. Next moment she could only remember putting her finger and trigger and pulling it. She didn't remove her finger even after whole magazine was emptied. Her bullets met their victims and all were dead in pool of blood. Second time she was finding God on her side. She did spit on face of Narayan, though he was dead. But that gave immense satisfaction to her. She cries aloud and fell on floor unconscious. When she regained consciousness she was in custody.

Her brother came to her in police station with Sargam in around midnight and wanted to engage best lawyer for her but she refused. He assured her that Sargam would be taken care as elder sister of Anuj. That was third time she was lucky.

Ghazal took promise from Nitiya not to write story as that would destroy many lives and that she shared her life to someone to acknowledge that goodness and hope also prevails in this world full of deceit. Nitiya also had good news for her. Suresh had met with accident in USA and his both legs were crushed and were removed and he is living now crippled life as he had also developed renal cancer. Ghazal asked her "How do you know him?" Reply came "I am his younger sister". And Nitiya left with a satisfied Ghazal looking upwards with speechless thanks to God, who was not good to her in life but at last who allowed her to die in peace.

□□□